ONE WOMAN

Barbara Mary Powe

ARTHUR H. STOCKWELL LTD.
Elms Court   Ilfracombe   Devon
Established 1898

© *Barbara Mary Powe, 1993*
First published in Great Britain, 1993

*All rights reserved.
No part of this publication may be reproduced
or transmitted in any form or by any means,
electronic or mechanical, including photocopy,
recording, or any information storage and
retrieval system, without permission
in writing from the copyright holder.*

*The story, characters and fictional
incidents in this book (autobiographical
material excluded) bear no relation to
actual persons, places or events.*

ISBN 0 7223 2780-3

*Printed in Great Britain by
Arthur H. Stockwell Ltd.
Elms Court   Ilfracombe
Devon*

Contents

Interlude in Rome	5
Miracle of Love	13
Assignment Undercover	18
Gorgeous Gigolo	40
Death by Slow Deprivation	52
One Woman's War	63
Poem — Blue Mountains' Ecstasy	71

To the Memory of

MY FATHER

"SIDERE MENS

EADEM MUTATO"

Interlude in Rome

I don't know whether it was the atmosphere in Rome, the balmy air, the scent of the familiar flowers, the canopies of hanging wistaria and the masses of azaleas, with bees buzzing in the gardens of the Villa Borghese — whatever it was, as I sat under the striped sun-umbrella in the Piazza della Repubblica, I felt this was home.

Certainly the coffee was more bitter, black and strong and the newspapers bore headlines in bold Italian print but it was the same. I might just as well be sitting in Martin Place with the perfume of the boronia and roses and stocks from the coloured wagons pervading the air and the headlines of the newspapers telling me the same world news as in Rome.

So I suppose I wasn't surprised when a handsome well-dressed man sat next to me. "Do you mind?" he asked.

"No," I nodded towards the vacant seat.

"Are you on vacation?"

"Yes," I replied.

He was speaking English, which he had learnt and I was speaking sometimes English, sometimes Italian which I had learnt, but it was the same, we were both speaking the language of the heart and we understood each other perfectly.

The Piazza della Repubblica was beautiful at that time of evening. The 4 p.m. siesta was over and the crowds had moved back into the square. The sun was making dappled shadows over the couples drinking peacefully in the warm summer evening. There was history in the air and stories behind each door facing the piazza.

"May I order you a Cinzano to drink with your coffee?" He smiled a warm Italian smile.

"Yes, thank you." I wasn't thinking too clearly, I was in a daze at the end of the lazy hot day.

"You are English?" he asked. "American?"

"No, Australian," I answered proudly.

His smile widened and his interest grew. "Australian. Yes, you have green eyes like the sea around Australia's coast and fair hair like the sand and a slightly sun-kissed complexion. But you are still fair and that is why I mistook you for being English. May I ask your name?"

"Frances. Frances Robinson. And yours?"

"Paolo," he confided, leaning forward and shaking my hand in a warm Italian greeting. "Paolo Rossini," he smiled with pride. "We have lived in Rome for many centuries. I would like to show you our beautiful city."

I shook my head. "My tour leaves Rome tomorrow morning."

His face clouded. "But no. We have only just met." He reached across the table and clasped my two hands in his. "Francesca, please don't go." He released one of my hands and pressed the other to his lips.

I noticed for the first time his deep brown eyes and his warm olive complexion, how well-groomed his thick black hair was, how thick and dark his eyebrows. His hands were manicured, his shirt white and immaculate, his tie straight, tiepin matching his cuff links, his dark suit tailored. Who was Paolo Rossini, merging before me into an ambassador for Rome, welcoming me into its history, its secrets, its life?

His eyes, his smile, the warmth of his hand were irresistible.

"Please don't leave, Francesca, now that I have just found you. Cancel your tour. Stay on for at least a day."

If this was Midsummer Night madness, well, what could I do? "I'll sleep on it," I said, meaning to walk back to the Hotel Albergo Sorrento and rejoin the tour.

He smiled. "Tonight is the open-air opera 'Aida', under the stars in the ruins of the Baths of Caracalla. Are you going to hear it?"

"Aida" under the stars! Memories came back of seeing the

opera in the Domain, lying on rugs on the lawn, sipping champagne cold from the ice, with the lights coming on around Sydney Harbour. There was nothing more memorable. And now "Aida" in Rome, under a northern sky. Oh, I couldn't miss it! I thrilled at the thought.

"Would you like me to buy tickets?"

"Come," he said, pressing my purse shut and we walked together to the box office.

With the tickets in his pocket, he turned to me. "Now we have the evening before us. Have you seen the Trevi Fountain floodlit?"

"Well, only this morning I threw a 50 cent coin into the fountain hoping, wishing to come back. But I have not seen it floodlit."

His steady arm under my arm moved to become his hand in mine.

"I hope you don't mind," he said and I felt a lilt of joy as we moved on through the crowds of shoppers, stopping to look at the kid gloves and silk scarves on display in the windows. We passed the Café Greco which Paolo told me had not changed since Byron and Wagner sat there.

Along the Via Condotti we wandered into a shop where Paolo inspected shoes. The smell of leather was heavenly. I looked at a pair which fitted perfectly and felt like kid gloves on my feet. I was frightened he was going to buy them for me so I put them back quickly and moved away.

He delayed for some time but I noticed he had a package when he came out. "Did you buy some shoes?" I asked.

He looked as pleased as the Cheshire Cat. "You are the traveller in Rome. You will need these," and he carelessly bundled them into my arm.

"But I can't accept these," I protested.

He blew a kiss. "They won't fit me. It's too late to take them back. They are a souvenir. Wear them and remember the time you walked with Paolo Rossini."

At the end of the Via Condotti was a small enclosed square and there it was! The renowned Trevi Fountain. The floodlights lit up the waterfalls cascading around King Neptune and his steeds on the façade of the Renaissance Palace.

Paolo sat on the edge with his back to the fountain and pulled me towards him playfully. Feeling his warm body against me, hard and masculine, yet gentle and kind, I felt that I had waded into the Trevi Fountain and was out of my depth. He was like a pleasant drug, a soporific which I felt I needed and possibly which I could not do without.

Everything shone more brightly because he was there. The fountain in the daytime had been very charming but now, held comfortably in Paolo's arms, I seemed to float in another dimension, filled with joy and a new love. The lights coming on seemed like glow-worms and Rome by night an enchanted cave filled with increasing delights and pleasures. I wondered in fact if something had been put in my drink or was it just romance?

"Come on and we'll have something to eat before the opera." He seemed amused at my bewildered state.

We dined at Da Pietro, by candlelight with chianti and a huge bowl of roses, fresh and fragrant. The soft music started and we danced while waiting for our meal.

"Tomorrow we will go to Silvi Marina, a beautiful fishing village on the Adriatic Coast. We'll have a picnic and you can swim if you like."

Now the reality of my situation became a little painful. I should go on with the tour tomorrow. Would I? Could I? The last question was the one I could not answer.

Paolo's will and Paolo's desire seemed to have taken over and Rome, exotic Rome, seemed to be luring me to stay. There would never be another Paolo and never again would I feel like this.

"Aida" was magical; the seats set among the old columns, the ruins of the ancient Baths of Caracalla cool, fanned by the evening breeze and the majesty of the performance with camels and horses and chariots racing across the stage, transported me to a world I shall never forget.

I felt Paolo's hand gripping mine firmly, possessively, passionately and I knew I would not be on the coach tomorrow morning.

When he brought me to my hotel and saw me safely to my door, he did not rush me. "The decision to stay or leave is yours, Francesca. You said you wanted to sleep and decide.

The coach, you say, leaves at 8.30 a.m. I shall be here at nine in the car. I will bring wine and something for the picnic, the rest we can buy in the hills. Don't forget your swimsuit. Goodnight,'' and lingering over my hand, he kissed it tenderly.

I staggered like a drunk into my room and lay on the bed in a dream. Whatever was happening? Whatever did happen? Tonight had been the best night of my life!

At 7.30 there was the usual knock at the door. "Time to get ready. We leave in one hour." But all I could think of was 9 o'clock and Paolo. I went out and saw the coach driver. I pleaded fatigue. I would join them later. I knew the itinerary. It was all right. The hotel was able to accommodate me.

It was a heavenly day. My aqua sundress and straw beach hat looked fresh and cool. My swimsuit fitted slimly underneath.

As I came out, there was Paolo's car parked opposite. His hand was shaking when he came forward to take my arm and squeezed it as if to make sure I was real. He said nothing but kept looking at me, smiling. His sleeves were rolled up to the elbow, his shirt a crisp blue striped cotton opened at the neck. His slacks were white linen.

We stopped in the piazza for some provisions. The Spanish Steps were a mass of baskets of flowers — poppies bobbing red and orange, late daffodils tossing their golden heads. Tubs of roses perfumed the air and jasmine twined around basket handles. At the foot of the Steps we paused to look on Keats' house, where he had died, and I remembered his Odes with nostalgia.

Next, for our picnic, a punnet of strawberries in season, delicious, and a cluster of rich red cherries, freshly-baked breadsticks, cheeses, salamis, olives, grapes and chianti.

We stepped into Paolo's white Alfa Romeo and then we were on our way out of the city over the Abruzzi Mountains to the Adriatic Coast.

The road to Pescara was dotted with little towns on the hills and in the distance snow glistened on the mountains. Large white oxen lazily worked on the cultivated slopes, crystal streams babbled over pebbles.

The green sea was inviting, clear and cold on the hot summer day. Why did it remind me of Clontarf Beach in Sydney, peaceful, dreamy and calm? It was so like home.

The day passed by dreamily and I remember falling asleep with Paolo's arm around me as we drove along the deserted roads through the peaceful countryside.

That night I wondered when the dream would burst.

But next morning it was still a reality. Off to Capri with Paolo driving down the magnificently terrifying Amalfi Drive. The road was very narrow as we came around the cliff top and looked down at the sheer drop below. As we swung around the blind bends I shut my eyes and held my breath. Paolo took his arm off the steering wheel to comfort me and I quickly assured him I was all right. After taking an extra deep breath, I began to relax and enjoy it all.

The magnificent vista took my breath away, revealing its splendour at each turn. The rugged mountain slopes to the right stretched down to the sea dotted with greenery, bushes nestling against the rock face and trees reaching out and up to the sky. Picturesque houses nestled among the trees gazing out on the spectacular view. Clusters of white villas occupied pride of place around the sea edge, the vivid pink of the climbing bougainvillea contrasting with the whitewashed walls and the vivid blue of the sea against a paler azure sky. Promenades and pebbled beaches dotted the foreshores. At each turn the sparkling sea changed from deep blue to clear aqua.

The wind in my face made me laugh, and as we came down from the heights I could smell the sparkling Mediterranean. Ahead, rugged rock formations jutted out into the sea with the mountains in the distance and a marina jutting out into the water. The peaceful sea was dotted with boats, and houses appeared here and there along the foreshore.

A whirlwind tour of Sorrento and Naples and then we were on the little canopied launch on our way to the resplendent Isle of Capri.

In no time we were transferred into one of the little rowing boats and the oarsman was trying to haul us via a rope into the large dark cave of the magnificent Blue Grotto. A strong wind was whipping up the waves and we had to wait for them to subside to enter the cave, splashed and laughing refreshed by the salt spray. Inside was a touch of Paradise. Here the water was indescribably phosphorescent blue. How I yearned to dive in and swim like a mermaid, but Paolo's restraining hand enabled me to sit still and drink in this delightful experience. Nature's beautiful blue phosphorescence excelled anything I have ever seen or will ever see again. Its excellence will inspire my mind forever.

"Oh, Paolo, I shall never forget this!"

"And I shall never forget you," he said.

The rest of the day was a dream. The Isle of Capri was idyllic. Marina Piccola flanked by several monoliths rising out of the sea, huge rock formations reminded me of the Three Sisters guarding Echo Point in the Blue Mountains.

The promenade took us to a picturesque bathing establishment with coloured dressing sheds, tables and chairs under striped sun-umbrellas and tubs of bright flowers around a built-in pool. Fragrant gardens and tree-lined drives gave glimpses of the villas as we took a drive along the seafront. The lovely villas, the bougainvillea, the sea reminded me of Sydney's peaceful Palm Beach, only more exotic. Pale clear green water lapped the pebbled beaches. It was wonderful! Wonderful!

The drive took us up to Anacapri past the Hotel Augustus with its dominant statue commanding the sea. Then we drove back down to Capri with its colourful shops, bright beachwear, large straw bags and hats, open-air restaurants nestled in cool greenery and a guitarist playing "Torn'a Sorrento", "Come back to Sorrento, or I must die!"

Then I understood the soul of Italy and knew that my love for Italy would never die.

That night, back in Rome, Paolo nodded as he watched me sip my Cinzano and I knew that this was to be our last time together. The Italian Ambassador had completed his work.

"This evening my wife, the Countess of Monte Verde, will return from her trip to Milano. My duties of State will begin again. Thank you, Francesca, for this taste of heaven we have shared," and he handed me a poem which he had written.

> *"A fleeting moment touched with gold,*
> *Two loves shared, secrets untold,*
> *Though we part, yearn not,*
> *Let the memories unfold."*

We stood up and slowly walked together to the church, "St. Peter in Chains, San Pietro in Vicoli", where we gazed at the ancient chains held in a glass case, a reminder that St. Peter was freed by a miracle from heaven.

From a dark niche the statue of Moses looked out on us, so lifelike the blood seemed to be pulsating through his veins. I shall never forget it.

Then Paolo took me to light a candle.

"Now I must leave you," he said. "Wherever you go on your way, Francesca, please think kindly of me and may the memory of this candle burn forever in your heart."

He was gone. The interlude in Rome was over.

But the candle burns on forever.

Miracle of Love

When I joined the queue from QANTAS Flight QF729 waiting to go through the barrier at Jakarta Airport, I felt butterflies in my stomach at the thought of meeting the seventeen-year-old Indonesian girl I had started sponsoring as a child seven years ago.

It had all started when my mothering instincts led me to sponsor a little girl overseas. The shock when I received the first photograph was so great that I immediately tore up the picture of that emaciated face with a hopeless expression showing the pain of life slipping away. My peace had gone and in its place began a dedication to work as hard as I could to send money over to support that child and keep her alive.

Her history card reads: *"Srisadarati was born in a small village in South Malang. Her father earns a poor living doing odd jobs. Her mother died of rheumatism. As her father is very weak and can no longer care for her any longer, she and her sister are living in the Tabita Home, while the brother lives with their father in a small bamboo hut. She is in the 2nd Grade at school, doing her best. Her health is poor as she suffers from malnutrition. We do hope that you would kindly accept the poor child into your family for further loving support, especially in prayer."*

And so my prayers started, the money flowed and each month I sent extra to see that she had vitamins and minerals in addition to daily care. Dear Australia, I remember how we sent biscuits filled with nourishment to Biafra and I hoped, oh how I hoped that this little soul would respond.

The next photo that arrived some months later showed a

little face less pinched with the same wide-set brown eyes and this time a slight tilt up of the chin, defiant against the poverty she lived in. Beside her stood her father, his open jacket revealing a sunken chest and protruding ribcage where each rib could be counted.

So my next savings, small as they were, went for her family.

A letter came back: *"My father thanks you deeply for the gift. He could repair our old house and he has married again so he is in good care."*

Slowly as each letter came in, I learnt more of this dear little girl. By some miracle our birthdays were the same month, so in advance I would send birthday money, and I have never enjoyed my birthdays so much waiting to hear what she had bought for her birthday gift: *"I have spent the money you sent me on one school bag, one blanket and one pair of sandals. I also bought some cookies and invited six friends. We had a wonderful time together. I shared the rest with my father so that he can buy the things that he needs daily. I also bought one school bag for my friend."*

My dear niece, Susan, was making a trip to Indonesia and kindly took a large toy koala bear which played "Waltzing Matilda" along with other gifts.

The letter came back: *"Indeed Srisadarati was filled with great joy as she received the toy koala bear. Besides that, all children here rejoiced with her as well. They all admired and loved the bear. As a matter of fact, it was already late at night so her superintendent took them all to bed. Srisadarati kept the bear in her bed and next morning all children played with it. Such a nice thing for them all to be able to see the bear singing! You do not have that animal in Indonesia!"*

The years passed, each photo showing a happier child than the last and school reports reading: *"Once again I am very happy to enclose the latest Progress Report on your sponsored child here in Indonesia. Another year has passed and your child has grown taller and entered a higher grade in school and is healthier because of your warm personal care."*

The activities included volleyball, ping-pong, reading, table games, gymnastics, drawing, embroidery, clay modelling, paper cutting, bamboo work and wood carving.

Domestic chores included cooking, helping in the kitchen and ironing clothes. Christian instruction included Church attendance, Bible study, choir and home devotions.

On her 16th birthday, her letter reads: *"I gladly received your birthday gift of $5.00 and I do thank you very much for your kindness. I spent the money on nice shoes and also cookies. And I am so happy. Hope you will enjoy my photo. Psalm 23 was read for me especially on my birthday party. I liked it very much. I know the Lord is my Shepherd and He will always help me. After prayers, we had a nice dinner on my birthday. Hope you will pray so that I can be successful in my study. Bye for now, dear. Thanks again. May God bless you abundantly. Love from Srisadarati."*

She did continue her study and it led to nursing school.

Well, I was given the opportunity to go on a tour of Indonesia and I made a detour to the Home.

In preparation I collected the ABC *"Learn Indonesian"* book and records and learnt a few phrases — *"Terima Kasi* — Thank You"; *"Salamat Malang* — Good Morning"; *"Salamat Siang* — Good Day"; *"Salamat Sore* — Good Evening".

And here I was on Indonesian soil at Jakarta Airport with a bag full of all the gifts I could think of. Simplicity rather than expense was the keynote I had been told, so I had children's books and coloured pencils for the young ones at the Home; sweets, books on Australian animals and Peach's Australia; my old battery-operated cassette player which I thought they might like to use, and a few packets of seeds which I had carefully checked with Customs, the Indonesian Embassy and the Department of Import and Export.

The loudspeakers blared, the armed guards directed us on our way. Once out of the city, like all cities, I began to live again. We travelled via mini Indonesia and the beautiful Bogor Botanical Gardens where they pick eucalyptus leaves for mosquito bites and clean their shoes with a flying seed! The frangipanni were so fragrant! On we went through tea plantations and Puncak Pass to beautiful Bandung where we dropped into the hotel swimming pool.

The next day we toured the sulphur volcano Tangkuban,

the Ciater tea plantation and hot springs, and I felt I had gone back a thousand years! The most beautiful peace descended upon me. It continued as the pace of life slowed down. The gentle white bullocks pulled their loads leisurely beside the road. The pickers in the tea plantations waved. It reminded me of my friends at home as we stopped work for the tea break and stood around the tea trolley to chat for a moment. And then it seemed that I could smell the fresh aroma of the Australian outdoor and tea boiling in the billy with eucalyptus leaves thrown in for good measure. I reached in my pocket for a packet of dried eucalyptus leaves a friend had given me as a *Bon Voyage* but I did not need them. Home was in the heart and here I felt at home and welcome.

The people and I laughed as we greeted each other, and when I used the phrases I had learnt and said *"Salamat Siang"* they pointed to the sun, the same sun seen from Australia as the rotating earth made its endless journey around it.

Walking down tracks in the woodlands was like walking along the Australian bush tracks. The people smiled and held up their children for me to admire. The language of love knows no barriers. The babies chewed on small corn cobs as the children at home teethed on rusks. As I looked at the little ones, I wondered how I would find Srisadarati, and how she would find me.

Her letters over the years had started by saying *"I have a doll named Buyung"* and later *"Here I am fine and happy. I love borrowing books from the school library. I enjoy reading story books about animals."* A plane flew overhead. I remembered she had written *"They told me that the planes which go through the village are going to Australia."*

Here transport was so different. Life seemed to pass slowly and peacefully, and it showed in the happy faces of the workers. It was the wet season and the farmers, busy in the rice fields, took time off to wave to us. It was humid but the rains meant that the plants, crops and flowers were alive and green. Certainly it was hotter than home but we wore cotton and had flasks of cooled boiled water from the hotel.

A tour of the hills was like driving along Mona Vale Road with stately trees on each side and not a house in sight as far as the eye could see. On top of the mountain was a delightful restaurant, a large wooden hut hidden amongst the greenery. From the open verandahs all around we gazed on a peaceful panorama of cool vines, pink hibiscus, cream and gold frangipanni and endless green trees reaching right down to the distant sea. I took a deep breath of fresh air and my heart beat with joy. The meal of satay vegetables with hot peanut sauce served by silent waiters was just as I remember it in my favourite Indonesian restaurant in Sydney.

The tour continued and then we were there!

The houseparents met us, and in the background was the whispering of the little children excited at their rare visitors. We sat down and Srisadarati came forward, demure, petite and slender for her seventeen years, and then she burst out in giggling and laughter and a smile I shall never forget! The memory of that haunting, emaciated face had gone forever and I laughed too. A miracle? Yes, a miracle of love!

We were served a sumptuous banquet, we sang, recording "Waltzing Matilda" on the cassette player which I left with them. We drove up into the hills to visit her family.

Her father was still alive, elderly and not well, but very dignified. Her stepmother showed us the pig she had bought and the piglets for trading, which meant they were indeed well-off, despite their bamboo hut bare on a stone floor and their sole coconut tree on a small block of land. But they were happy with all their neighbours crowding around smiling.

A young man came up and held Srisadarati's hand, and I knew her future was assured.

Srisadarati has now turned eighteen and has left the programme.

As I look at the beautifully worked sampler and lace collar which she gave me as a souvenir and at the Christmas card with Christ in the manger and children of all nations worshipping Him *"Mari Kita Men Yembah Dia* — Come let us adore Him!", I understand perfectly those wonderful words "Blessed are the peacemakers, for they shall be called the children of God".

Assignment Undercover

In 1942, at the height of World War II, under the Nazi regime, the Berlin Union of Businessmen and Industrialists signed the initial document for the European Economic Community. What does this mean for the world? Is this salvation for the peoples of Europe or a Nazi plot? Time will tell. In any event good comes out of evil. World Wars I and II, started by Germany, have been won. Wisdom again will prevail.

The EEC was ratified when France joined Germany in April 1951, signing the European Coal and Steel Community Treaty of Paris. The dream of European unity was becoming a reality. The signing of the Treaty of Rome on 25th March, 1957, established the Common Market on a firm basis. In time the membership would grow, twelve nations by 1986. Would there be future unity or disunity?

In April 1951, while the Treaty of Paris was being signed, in all ignorance of its implications, I was enjoying my French connections with the Messageries Maritimes, the French Shipping Company in Sydney, Australia.

As I sailed up the Lane Cove River from my home in Northwood to Circular Quay on the little ferry *La Radar*, my *joie de vivre* knew no bounds. Porpoises played under the prow, diving and surfacing to blow bubbles of fun at us in the sparkling foam. As soon as the ferry reached Long Nose Point they left us finding Circular Quay too busy and the deep green water sometimes too coloured with oil slicks.

A lot of water had passed under the bridge, dear Sydney Harbour Bridge, since the end of the war. The memories came back as we passed little Fort Dennison alone in the middle of Sydney Harbour to protect us. All was dark during the blackouts, except for the little Bondi tram with all her lights on, impervious to the danger that she was a beacon lighting up the coast to Watsons Bay on South Head faithfully depositing passengers all along the way.

The Managing Director and all at the Messageries Maritimes were delighted that France had signed the Treaty of Paris. It was a brilliant venture. No more would Germany be able to start up a war, all Europe would be united together, it would be Utopia.

However, one Frenchman in the office did not join in the exuberance. M. le Pain, the accountant from Paris, who wore dark horn-rimmed glasses, looked sombre. "With Germany instigating this, no good will come of it. You mark my words" and with a puff of cigar smoke, he stormed out of the building. Later I learnt he had been to see his good friend M. Marc le Blanc at the Comptoir National d'Escompte de Paris, the French Bank in Sydney.

That night there was a celebratory dinner on board *La Polynesie*, the little passenger/cargo ship which had just returned from the New Hebrides. The menu was superb. The cordon bleu chef excelled himself. Hors d'oeuvres consisted mainly of seafood delicacies; roulades of smoked salmon, shrimps mariette, prawn croquettes, anchovies supremes, lobster cassolettes, all this with avocado savouries, paté de foie gras and caviar. The main meal was venison either grenadins or sauté St. Hubert with a choice of chateaubriand or coq au vin. Desserts were a delight — croquembouche, profiteroles, bombes and parfaits. Coffee and liqueurs were served with fresh strawberries dipped in glistening toffee and assorted chocolates. *Bon appetit!*

The stars had never shone so brightly over Sydney Harbour as that night. They were like sparkling diamonds on black velvet reflected on the deep green water in a shimmering pathway of moonbeams. My escort, Alex, who had grown up with me at Northwood, looked handsome in his grey tuxedo with maroon lapels. Together we danced beautifully, my long pink taffeta frock swirling over the deck as we pivoted to Woody Herman's "Golden Wedding" and glided to "La

Bomba". The river and harbour had always called us romantically together and tonight opened up a wonderful future for us. *La Dolce Vita!* How does one say that in French? What does it matter. The war is over. Life is sweet.

But is the war over? Back in those halcyon days of Summer 1951, little did I know how fate would lead me in mysterious ways.

In the meantime, life was to be enjoyed. We swam and paddled in his small canoe, until one day it spilled us out into the middle of Woodford Bay, to sink or swim. Longueville opposite was such a long way across, to go back to Northwood was even further and so we swam, and swam and swam till our toes touched down on the creamy white sand on the opposite shore. Armies of blue soldier crabs scuttled away as we sat and shook the salt water out of our hair and laughed and kissed and revelled at just being alive and young — sixteen years, sweet sixteen!

We would spend days at Avalon Beach and nights at parties. Together we bicycled to the Lane Cove National Park, swam and barbecued with friends. We played tennis, took boats out on Coal and Candle Creek and grilled the fish we had caught on hot coals to be smothered in garlic butter and fresh tartare sauce. We dined on exotic European cuisine and watched the imported French films at the Savoy. We ate spicy curries at Martha Washington's in Martin Place and went up to the Prince Edward Theatre, walking under the gleaming chandeliers to compare that film with *"Marius, Cesar et Fanny"* or *"Les Enfants du Paradis"*.

There is something about peace, after a war. It is like coming out of a cocoon, a fresh crysallis, a fresh start. Although it was now the sixth year after Victory in Europe and very importantly for us in Australia, Victory in the Pacific, there was still a hesitancy about too great a celebration. After all, the New Look, letting your skirts down, splashing out on yards of material as a reaction to the clothing coupons, hadn't really been such a success.

Alex and I decided there were better ways to celebrate life. We dreamt of joining the Diplomatic Corps, travelling to Europe as Australian Ambassadors to solve the world's problems. In 1951 in Australia there were no problems. Life was a breeze.

We practised our languages together. Alex would quote Heinrich Heine, gazing into my eyes, telling me they were like blue cornflowers against my hair, gold like wheat.

"Du bist wie eine Blume
So hold und schön und rein.
Ich schau dich an und Wehmut
Was kommt im Herz hinein."

And I would long to sail with him out beyond the Pacific Ocean to the Mediterranean Sea, to swim in the Blue Grotto and let its phosphorescent blue water caress me like a mermaid. How I loved the sea! I would sing like Charles Trenet — *"La mer a bercé mon coeur, pour la vie!"*

We encouraged each other all through our studies at Sydney University, until in 1954, we both graduated with distinctions. Alex was first to be given a posting to Vienna, Assistant to the Australian Consul General. Many tears flowed as he flew out on the huge Qantas jet.

Although I had asked to be near him, I was shortly after appointed to the Australian Embassy in Rome. While I would have preferred Paris, my Italian studies shone, so I was posted to the Eternal City. While there I planned on holidays to go to Florence and walk in the footsteps of Dante Alighieri —

"Nel mezzo del cammin di nostra vita . . . ."

In summer I would motor down the Amalfi Drive to Naples and over to the Isle of Capri and visit Gracie Fields' house. There was so much I would do.

In the meantime, duty called, business before pleasure, *noblesse oblige.*

At the airport, on the day of my departure, I was approached by M. le Pain from the Messageries Maritimes. This time his horn-rimmed glasses accentuated the intensity of his dark brown eyes. He seemed to look right into my mind.

"Bon voyage, Mademoiselle et bonne chance. I believe you will be spending a week in Paris before taking up your appointment in Rome. M. Marc le Blanc has returned to the Bank in Paris and has urgently contacted me to give you his

address. He wishes you to telephone him as soon as you arrive, on a matter of national importance."

A hint of intrigue accompanied his words.

The address was handed to me on a neat business card.

"*Au revoir, Mademoiselle et bonne chance!*"

"Good luck!" Why had he said it that way with a hint of hidden meaning? What were the implications of this meeting?

It was April, glorious Spring when I arrived in Paris and I bought a huge bunch of daffodils which I took to the Hotel M. le Prince where I was staying, and put them on the dressing table of my small room. From my balcony I looked down on the flower seller, wheeling a small white handcart with all Spring flowers a blaze of colour spilling over the sides. The fragrance of stock filled the air, overpowering the more delicate perfume of soft pink roses and little sprays of lily of the valley. The masses of daffodils were reminiscent of Wordsworth:—

> "I wandered lonely as a cloud
> That floats on high o'er vale and hills,
> When all at once I saw a crowd, —
> A host of golden daffodils"

It reminded me so much of the beautiful Blue Mountains back home where there were fields of golden correopsis all along the Great Western Highway and railway line right up to Mt. Victoria and beyond. Nostalgia! Yet who could be sad or reminiscent here in Paris with the red trolleybuses bustling past, and snatches of the latest fashions to attract one's gaze and imagination.

As I sat under a brightly-striped sun-umbrella on the Boulevarde sipping a *café au lait* and enjoying a *petit four*, I remembered that M. Marc le Blanc wished to have a rendezvous. Why not? The telephone was brought to my table. "M. le Blanc?"

"*Oui, Mademoiselle, je viens tout de suite.*"

Before I knew it, M. le Blanc, who insisted I call him Marc, was beside me, almost unrecognizable now he was with the Comptoir National d'Escompte de Paris Head Office, resplendent in a Pierre Cardin suit and to my amazement, carrying a cane. Later it surprised me that he used a monocle to read the important document he produced so very mysteriously.

"My dear, it is very fortuitous that you should be in Paris, right at this time." He smiled.

'Yes' I thought, 'the sun is streaming down on the little coffee tables here on the Boulevarde shaded by little striped awnings and red and white sun-umbrellas.'

"Very fortuitous" his voice honed in.

Up above the sky was a cloudless blue. There were two pigeons fighting over a piece of croissant and I longed to throw them the last of my little cake, it was so rich.

"To translate for us the German documents into French, with the utmost secrecy would entail a handsome retainer."

He thrust before me a paper with a sum of French francs which swam before my eyes.

"The fact that you will be in Rome, away from it all, makes it so much more fortuitous. There is a regular courier service and the documents will be returned by you as if coming from the Australian Embassy there, on normal official business. Have you an answer, my dear?"

Why hadn't I listened more closely? Translating documents from German into French? Why not? As I had the best dictionaries, I could see no problems.

His hand slid over mine. "You will be doing a great service to France. We must know just what the plot is all about. Forewarned is forearmed. If we had no concerns, of course, this would not be necessary, but, we have received information emanating from Berlin, that relates to the initial Union of Businessmen and Industrialists, which we find very disturbing, alarming in fact. This European Economic Community and France's initial role in becoming the first partner with Germany at the helm of this bureaucracy, needs a lot more understanding. Are Germany's motives pure? Or is it another *'Deutschland über alles'* — 'Germany over all' mentality as in the First and Second World Wars? Do you comprehend my meaning?"

Now I was reminded of my father's words — "Don't trust Nazi Germany. Naziism is not dead, it has just gone underground and it will raise its ugly head again." His words had made me shudder. On the Newsreels I had seen the thundering of Nazi Gestapo jackboots as they intoned *"Sieg Heil! Sieg Heil! Sieg Heil!"* along the streets of Nürnberg and then Auschwitz, and what followed was too horrific to recall.

"Will you do the translations for us, confidentially? There will be no contact, just the courier calling at your Australian Embassy in Rome, bringing you a cheque from us."

He waited, looking at me intently. There was an urgency in his dark brown eyes, which I did not understand at the time.

"Yes" my voice came out as a whisper. I took courage. "Yes" I said boldly. The clandestine agreement had been made.

Carefully he took a form from an envelope in his briefcase. It was easy to read. I was to sign as translator for an agreed sum, with freedom to terminate on either side.

"Of course you realize the confidentiality of this undertaking. You must speak to nobody about the work you are doing. You will be completely alone. If your work is good and always on time, there will be a bonus for you. *C'est entendu?*"

"*Oui, M. le Blanc.*"

We shook hands. He gripped my hand tightly.

"The first assignment will arrive when you have taken up your appointment in Rome, next week. *Au revoir, Mademoiselle, merci bien et bonne chance!*"

He turned his back and was gone.

A cold chill slid down my back. What had I let myself in for? Good luck! Why had he said it that way? Why should I need Good Luck?

The afternoon sunshine was slipping from the tables along the deserted place, and I drew my light jacket around me as I walked to the busy street where office workers were leaving their bureaux and hurrying home on the trolleybuses.

L'Hotel M. le Prince was quite cosy. The concierge, a petite motherly soul, seemed quite thrilled to have an Australian staying there. The meals were good and I saved my meat and fish scraps for her tortoiseshell cat, Mimi, who purred and rubbed against my legs. It was nice to have a bit of conversation but I was always aware that Mme. la Concierge was always listening for a piece of conversation that would prove worthwhile information to pass on to her wayward nephew, Raoul, who in turn would pass it down the line to his friends. This was a training period to keep my mouth shut so that when I arrived to work for the Embassy in Rome, I would not be indiscreet and let slip any information that would undermine any plan the Embassy was keeping secret or anything I was translating about the EEC.

Should I keep a diary? The information I received would weigh heavily on my mind. A diary might slip into the wrong hands. No, I would just have to tuck what I should learn away in the stronghold of my mind and let it fade and be forgotten.

But what of the distress of all this? Well, there would be someone at the receiving end of my translations whose responsibility it would be to deal with it all. Leave it to them.

A week in Paris. "Her trees were deck'd with Spring". The boutiques were gorgeous. First I would buy a cool Spring frock. Navy and white fine spots and stripes were à la mode and fuchsia pink in silk scarves, gloves, petits corsages of pink roses, pink sun-umbrellas and even pink attaché cases. *"C'est la vie"* — business with pleasure. Les rues de Paris were fragrant with Spring flowers and I sauntered back to l'Hotel M. le Prince swinging my parcels with *joie de vivre*.

That night I dined with two Australian friends who were touring the continent on a budget so we ate at a cheap restaurant, l'Auberge.

"When do you start at the Embassy in Rome?"

"Next Monday."

"We'll come and see you. We'll be in Italy in May. We'll drink a vino together. What are you doing tomorrow?"

We agreed to visit the splendid Palais de Versailles, enjoying the spacious grounds and revelling in a conducted tour of the apartments. If only this splendid age of royalty would return?

Then it was on to Montmartre to buy tickets for the Folies Bergères. The days passed delightfully. We visited Notre-Dame's Gothic Cathedral resplendent with stained glass windows secure on an island like a huge Noah's ark surrounded by water. At the flower market I bought huge bunches of Spring blossoms for Mme. la Concierge and for my own room at l'Hotel M. le Prince. Then we went on to the impressive Palais de Justice and S. Chapel with brilliant stained glass windows forming magnificent walls. By the Métro, we visited La Place de la Concorde with the Tuileries Gardens on the left, along the avenue to the fountain and obelisk in the centre. We caught a bus down the Champs Elysées to la Place de l'Etoile with the Arc de Triomphe and the burning flame in the centre surrounded by tributes of floral wreaths.

The Métro took us to the Eiffel Tower, up to the third floor with a magnificent view of all of Paris, the Place de l'Etoile radiating out like a star flanked with tree-lined boulevardes. From my binoculars I was sure I could see the little flower seller and her brightly-painted handcart filled with golden daffodils, now perfuming the air way down there on the Champs Elysées.

At long last I was able to visit Le Louvre and gazed at the Venus de Milo and the Mona Lisa smiling enigmatically. These and all the other magnificent works were breathtaking. History spoke volumes. That night we spent at L'Opera, exquisite theatre with indescribable décor, brilliant chandelier gracing the artistry and gold figures on ceiling and pillars, divine downstairs lobby and staircase with four magnificent statues. Tosca came to life, an unforgettable experience.

The next night, Alex flew in from Vienna. We held hands over a candlelit dinner.

"You know, I met a marvellous fellow in Vienna" he said, "a friend of the Habsburgs. He was telling me they lost everything in the last war. They're a very talented family, descended from Charlemagne, you know."

"No, I didn't know."

"Charlemagne was born way back in the 8th Century, Charles the Great, a huge man seven feet tall, great in stature and great in character. He was a marvellous emperor, powerful and warmhearted. *Rex Pater Europae*, 'King Father of Europe'. It was Charlemagne who Christianized the German Saxons, with the sword and then united twelve different nations into a United Europe. The Pope crowned him "Emperor". His capital is the German city of Aix-la-Chapelle and he was patron of learning and the Arts. Many people think we should follow in his footsteps with a United

Europe today. But where is Charlemagne to lead us?''

A petite waitress in miniskirt and mini top interrupted us, leaning over Alex invitingly. *"À votre service"* she smiled temptingly.

"Paris! It hasn't changed. Oh that all the restaurants were like this!" Alex looked relaxed.

"Well, I haven't noticed, but then I suppose it is the suave waiters who draw my attention mostly."

"*Touché*. Anyway, going back to the Habsburgs. My friend was telling me, after Otto the Great in 962, Germany went through *'Die Kaiserlose, schreckliche Zeit'* — 'the terrible time without an Emperor'. Then a succession of Habsburgs came and went. Rudolf of Habsburg from Austria brought prosperity, then later Albert II of Austria as King of Germany. It's interesting. When the Habsburg Frederick III became German King and was crowned Holy Roman Emperor, he introduced a Royal Monogram — A E I O U — *'Austriae est imperare orbi universo'* — 'All the world is subject to Austria'."

"I thought we were worried about Germany wanting all power — *'Deutschland über alles'*."

"Well, don't forget, Adolf Hitler was in fact an Austrian, an Austrian house painter. He was of course a bad 'un, showing his real colours ending up as a cowardly suicide in his bunker. A bit like Judas. Those people never last."

"Well, who else was there?"

"Napoleon Bonaparte crowned himself a second time with the 'Iron Crown' worn by Charlemagne wanting a United States of Europe under France. Otto the Great and others have all envisaged a United Europe."

"Well I prefer Sir Winston Churchill — 'blood, toil, tears and sweat'. He won the war and the support of the people. He was compassionate and a man of great foresight. He gave us the Victory sign.

"Yes, Hitler and Mussolini were no match for the Allies. It will be interesting to see who comes up next. It's funny how wars start. World War I was triggered by the assassination of Archduke Francis Ferdinand, heir to the throne of Austria-Hungary, by a Serbian in the Balkan town of Sarajevo. Funny if history repeats itself."

"Well, we don't want another Hitler. Tell me about him."

"When Germany was defeated in World War I and became a Republic, Hitler and others were embittered by the Treaty of Versailles, possibly rightly so. He became President of the NSDAP, National Socialist German Workers' Party. As a corporal he won the Iron Cross for personal bravery. He emulated Mussolini who wanted Rome as the centre of Western civilization and like Julius Caesar abolished the handshake for the old Roman salute with raised arm."

"The heil Hitler, you mean."

"Yes. He saw himself as the head of the German 'master race'. He took advantage of the economic turmoil, six million unemployed, all of which had been manipulated, and promised 'Lebensraum'. The National Socialist (Nazi) Party gained support and Hitler was asked to form a government, the Third Reich with Nazis taking complete control of Germany. Hitler thought one day he would rule all of Europe, and from there, the world. Adolf Hitler, the Austrian house painter, compared himself with Charlemagne, Frederick the Great and Napoleon. He sat himself in his mountain fortress in Obersalzberg surveying all. Legend tells that Charlemagne still sleeps in this mountain and will one day arise to restore the past glory of the German Empire."

"Yes, Charlemagne was a good man."

"While Hitler, who was a Catholic, was denounced by the Catholic Church because Naziism is anti-Christian. It's interesting bringing history up to date. In May 1939 Hitler and Mussolini signed 'The Pact of Steel'. On 1st September 1939, Hitler attacked Poland; World War II had begun, Hitler wanting to gain mastery of the world. In 1941 he made Napoleon's disastrous mistake of invading Russia, culminating in his defeat and suicide in April 1945, his ideals of a United States of Europe shattered."

"And yet the dream of a United Europe goes on."

"My friend is delighted with the Treaty of Paris signed just now, April 1951, to amalgamate French and German iron, coal, and steel resources, which will extend to Italy, Belgium, the Netherlands, Luxemburg and so on. They are planning a

Treaty of Rome in 1957 to create the Common Market, the EEC. West Germany as the centre of the European continent will be the most powerful. It all sounds like some man-made dream, history repeating itself, and yet Habsburg and many others believe the world will only be united in Christ, as the Bible tells us in Revelation 17:14 and elsewhere. He hopes the monarchy around the world will be restored. The Schönbrunn Palace he showed me is magnificent, ornate gold spacious rooms and grounds stretching as far as the eye can see with fountains, palm house and delightful environs. You must come over next holidays. You'd love the Vienna Woods."

Night had settled over Paris and many of the city lights had blinked out. Alex and I farewelled the romantic city together. Our memories will live on forever.

In a matter of days I had farewelled la belle Paris and the lights of Rome's Fiumicino's airport were blinking up at me.

On Monday morning I entered the doors of the Australian Embassy. *La dolce vita!* It was somebody's birthday and balloons and cake had taken over the office atmosphere. Everyone seemed to be young, and all were comparing notes of where they had spent their weekend. One couple had dined on rock melon and Parmesan ham, saltimbocca alla Romana and tartufi, high up in the mountains of Rocca di Papa overlooking the volcanic crater sparkling with crystal clear blue water. Others had been to the beaches at Ostia and Fregene. It reminded me of home in Australia, spending the weekends at Avalon or Newport, coming to work with a golden suntan and the added memory of salt sea breezes and the rhythmic sound of sea-green breakers capped with white foam, rolling up on the golden sand.

That night I was taken to see the opera "Aida" where we sat among the ruined columns of the Baths of Caracalla under a velvet sky studded with sparkling stars while a huge cast, accompanied by three horses and chariot, two camels and authentic Egyptians, with dazzling gold and red costumes, transported us to a faraway world and the charm of "Celeste Aida".

"You'll love Rome" my friends from the Embassy assured

me as we drank coffees and liqueurs at La Capricciosa. The days are balmy, Italians are romantic and know how to enjoy life. Of a Sunday you can sit al fresco at little coffee tables under bright sun-umbrellas beside tubs of pelargoniums and brilliant cerise bougainvillea, and just watch the people parade in the latest of fashions. Young lovers look as though they are waiting for the photographers to picture them in the latest social magazines.

Really the Embassy staff were a friendly, vivacious crowd. The days were busy liaising with Italians who didn't speak English, and Australians calling in at the Embassy re their lost passports, running out of money and so on.

It was only when a silent, sour-faced courier handed me a package marked *"Miss Felicity Harrison — Private and Strictly Confidential"* that my heart sank, remembering my promise to accept this mission.

The night seemed colder and darker as I left the Embassy at 8 o'clock that night, telling nobody of my responsibility. There were gusts of wind, whisking papers and leaves between the chairs and tables in the Piazza and a dark figure moved stealthily behind a blue door opposite. It looked like Raoul. Why was my imagination playing tricks?

When I reached my apartment I locked my door very carefully, making doubly sure the chain was fixed in place. Again a chill ran down my spine. Previously I had promised myself never to drink alone, but the chill would not go away so I brewed some coffee and added a good nip of whisky. Then I felt better.

Well, there was no time like the present. I sat down and opened the envelope: *"Mademoiselle, as soon as possible, if you don't mind, by Sunday at the latest. Telephone this number and the courier will come immediately, with your cheque."*

That was all, brief and businesslike.

The first translation was easy — a document outlining the agreement between Germany and France to pool German and French iron, coal and steel resources. Later Belgium, Luxemburg, the Netherlands and Italy would join. (At this time I was not to know that the European Economic Community or Common Market would be established with the signing of the Treaty of Rome on 25th March 1957 and by 1986 there would be twelve member nations.)

In ignorance I translated the innocuous document. What a good idea — a United Europe. West Germany, in the centre of Europe, becomes the most powerful nation as the core.

The next was a letter handwritten by a German official to a top Executive of the Bundesbank, strictly confidential and hand delivered. How my informant had managed to photocopy it, goodness knows, spies spying on spies, a network within a network.

The French, being in agreement with Germany, expected all communications to be shared, but from this it seemed that Germany was working alone, as some mastermind to control the EEC and then the world.

The cold shudders I had been experiencing were well founded.

The letter started in jocular vein: *"We are on top, they are eating out of our hands"* and so the System began to be revealed. From the Bundesbank the Banks throughout the world were to be undermined, lose customers' confidence, discredit the system and then . . .

I had to wait for the next courier's delivery.

My hands were perspiring. However, it was none of my business. The translation had been done, so I telephoned the courier. He would come immediately although it was after midnight.

When the door bell rang I leapt nervously envisaging some evil Nazi standing with a shotgun for betraying them. The courier looked just as sour as before yet I was pleased to wish him "Good Evening!" and dispose of the documents as soon as possible.

He smiled for the first time. *"Je vous remerçie mille fois —* a thousand thanks" he said in immaculate French, and he meant it.

He handed me my cheque from le Comptoir National d'Escompte de Paris, bowed politely, kissed my hand and left.

My sigh of relief brought the little tabby cat which I kept as my pet in the apartment, rubbing around my legs. She was warm and comforting as I picked her up and poured out fresh milk for her and a glass for myself, and then into bed.

The first assignment was over.

The next day the Consul General approached me to see if the apartment was to my liking.

Really I couldn't ask for better. It was ideally located in Via Francesco Massi in the fashionable part of Monteverde Vecchio and yet bordered on the new area where there were supermarkets and everything needed for the modern way of life. Truly it was delightful, a rooftop apartment with sole use of this sun deck with white painted pots of purple and cerise bougainvillea and bright golden yellow violas with purple upper petals spilling out of flower boxes. In the centre of the patio was a magnificent bay tree in a huge green tub with fresh garden herbs, oregano, basil, marjoram and fragrant mint cascading down the sides. Deck chairs and *chaise-longue* were shaded by a cool green-fringed sun-umbrella. A panoramic view stretched out over the whole of Rome. It was majestic. *La dolce vita!*

Inside the apartment was cool with marble floors. However, the bath was a surprise, a unique split-level affair where you sat with your feet on the lower level and the warm water lapping around your hips as though sitting in a chair in the sea. If the bath were filled too full, the water ran out for the rest of the apartment, so it was always a major performance not to be undertaken lightly. The electricity was not much better. Two or more appliances switched on was likely to fuse the whole apartment. One had to think very economically before preparing a meal and the thought of entertaining friends to a banquet was a real challenge. The warm, cosy heaters standing in the hall, lounge room and bedrooms were hot water heated. On the beautiful tiled floors, one felt like dancing life away.

When Saturday came, friends from the Embassy and I went exploring the glorious Villa Borghese. The gardens reminded me of home in Sydney, canopies of fragrant wistaria, masses of pink and white azaleas, bright purple, pink and white cinerarias and vivid bougainvilleas. The statues of The Rape of Persephone and Paolina Bonaparte were so lifelike, you felt their presence pervaded the empty rooms. The carved columns, gilt friezes and marbled floors were exquisite, unable to be forgotten. Two priests in vivid red cassocks wished us *"Buon Giorno"* as we strolled out onto the streets again.

Small Italian Fiats and motor scooters buzzed around noisily, and in the distance the huge Colosseum rose imposingly emanating history, the old and the new blended in a romantic atmosphere of eternity. The voices of the gladiators and the cries of the past still filled the air along with the noisy cries of the spectators swirling on the wind.

From the Forum, with its ruined columns rising from chipped tiled paved yards now overgrown with long green grass, came the whisperings of important men in togas carrying on the business of the day with learned scrolls tucked under their arms. The wind rustled and a minute figure stirred from the atrium. Was it a spectre from the past or just a figment of the imagination? My sigh dissipated into the breeze and was lost along with the whisperings of bygone days.

Sunday dawned another glorious Spring day. My friends from the Embassy decided I must see the Trevi Fountain. One of the girls was about to return to Australia and had to throw a coin in to make sure she came back again. The fountain, I had imagined to be sited in a huge Piazza, was tucked away at the end of the Via Condotti, a short narrow street with magnificent shops selling kid gloves and leather goods that were heavenly. This narrow lane barely opened into a tiny Piazza and squeezed in there was the resplendent Trevi Fountain carved in all its glory and telling an old, old story with the memory of its sculptor crawling in the shadows to finish his masterpiece which was to bring about his death working so long in the underground waterways saturating his lungs with its dampness. His memorial, his tribute gives so much pleasure to the living, perhaps the sacrifice was worth it all.

Then we went on to the beautiful St. Andrew's Presbyterian Church, through the pebbled courtyard, its path bordered with brightly-coloured flowers in pots. Inside, the pale-blue walls and ceilings embossed in white with beautiful oak panelling lent such a sense of peace that here seemed to be a touch of heaven itself. The open grave, the victory of Jesus Christ over death twenty centuries ago, reminded one to look to Christ the prize as St. Paul wrote: "I press toward the mark for the prize of the high calling of God in Christ Jesus" in his Letter to the Philippians.

The Catacombs of St. Calixtus, S. Callisto, were such a contrast. Here five floors underground were 90,000 tombs, miles of corridors where little children were buried on the corners with the dove of peace, altars and paintings and little candles. The victory over death seemed forgotten down here underground in the tombs. Even more depressing were the Catacombs of S. Sebastiano with 174,000 tombs, 100 feet deep, 5 floors and 8 miles of corridors. In the church was preserved the footprint of Christ, or so we were told.

To complete this macabre tour, we went along the Via Veneto to the Church of the Cappuchins with cemetery beneath where the bones and skulls were artistically arranged, even used to form a chandelier. Some of the bodies were placed upright, others lying down, some having been there since the 16th Century. Little crosses in the earth confirmed their faith.

Somehow I was in a very melancholy mood when I returned to the Embassy after the weekend. There was a large envelope waiting for me: *"Brava, Signorina! Well done! Your first assignment cheque includes a bonus. Please continue in the same way and the victory will be sweet."*

My heart sank. All day I planned how I could be free of my responsibility. Who else could or would do it for me? Nobody else. Really I was only a small link, a very small link in the chain. Perhaps one day I would be freed like St. Paul whose chains fell off. What was the word he used for the "mark", the destination, the finish of the race — Christ the prize. So I sat down that night, resigned to start, middle and finish. The start had taken place. Who knew when the marathon would finish?

As I worked on into the night, I became more depressed. Instead of a New World Order to save mankind, it transpired that some Nazi plot was hatching, not freedom for all but

"*Deutschland über alles* — Germany over all". Was not this what we had fought against in World Wars I and II? The domination of one nation over all was absolutely unacceptable. Nazi — the memories flooded back and I shuddered.

As I translated, the German words kept repeating themselves — "*die Zahl*", "the talon", which would scratch the "mark", the electronic mark, in numbers on people's hands or foreheads with invisible laser beam and numbers visible by way of satanic parallel lines, the bar code on all products, to link up a fiendish system. Already children were being coaxed to have paintings on their faces so as not to be frightened when the laser came. "The mark", the electronic mark would control people, all peoples of the earth unless they overcame it. As soon as the money was taken away, this was the only alternative. How beastly! Who did they think they were? Information on every person would be fed ultimately into the giant computer in Brussels, already the blueprint was nicknamed "the beast".

On and on I translated. The nations of the world would all be forced into debt and then the domino effect, one after another would fall and the World Bank would take over, not with currency, too fiddling like Nero as Rome burned, but a system that was redolent of the marking or numbering of the Jews, controlling them and exterminating them in the ovens of the concentration camps, the holocaust. Horrible! But this was worse, not death but complete control, electronic control, like robots in slavery to a Nazi dictator, people reduced to robots, never to be free.

Where was our Saviour now? What about His good plan for hope for the future? At least by exposing the enemy's plot, it was something to work against, to overcome.

And so the plot thickened. It would be explained to people how much more simple, easy, oh so easy it would be to have an invisible, indelible mark made up of three blocks of six numbers comprising the person's birthdate, place of residence and National Identification Number, conveniently tattooed on the hand or forehead, to be picked up with a laser rod . . .

How could I go on? A normal person's mind could not comprehend. So I closed the translation before me. It was too much.

Tabitha, the little tabby cat, jumped onto my lap. Her fur was soft and comforting. Her purr rumbled contentedly.

The clock showed 11 p.m. My stress was so great, the only thing to do was munch on carrots. This was something I had learnt during the war when we had been sent to the Blue Mountains as children for safety. Air-raid drill was carried out, and wooden pegs were hung around our necks to bite on to protect our teeth from shattering if the shells came. Carrots were so much better to bite on and chew later, good for the heart. *"Coraggio Signorina"* I had learnt in my Italian studies, so I put my head down again.

Money. Money was being phased out. Surely this was wrong. People were going to be left powerless, or so the powers behind this plot wanted. Then it would be demonic control.

Was this science fiction I was reading, all in the guise of unity, free economic community for all? Now that I was beginning to see what was behind it all, there was no way I ever wanted such a system, and yet the powers that be all thought it a great idea. But then so had people with Hitler, until he was exposed as an inhuman megalomaniac. This however was worse. The system being introduced was everything evil. How were human beings to be protected from it?

Translate. Translate. Translate. That was all I could do. This was my job. I must become detached. Somebody else had it all in hand. Translate, and so I did.

"Wir werden mit Australien erst . . ."

"We will start with Australia . . ."

Start what? What was going on? It was like a surgeon suddenly having a relative put on the operating table before him, the victim of a horrific accident and he had to use his skills, as always, perfectly, impassionately, until the job was done.

And so I translated. Now it had to be done, perfectly, to the very best of my ability. Later I would have a delayed reaction, but not now. The work had to be done.

The plot thickened. Buildings were to go up, buildings with

all the equipment needed, some near hospitals where the people would be marked with the laser beam, "the mark of the beast". This was what it was, the beast, the giant computer in Brussels controlling all. But who, who was the mastermind behind all this?

It was horrific. The words went on.

Six numbers. Six numbers. Six numbers — Birthdate. Location. National Security Number.

Once the people are marked, the electronic control will make them remote control robots in our System. We will re-educate them and they will all do our will. What a Utopia!

Who was this monster whose evil mind was trying to master the free world?

No way! I shut the file. No way!

It was after midnight. The clock ticked on, only a few more pages to be done. Cold shudders ran down my shoulders and arms. Could I write on? Tabitha purred contentedly on the rug over on the chair. "Miaow!" I picked her up and held her close to my cheek. She purred. My heart started up again.

Drink hot milk. Yes, I needed hot milk. Eat a carrot for my nerves. I did that. And then I was calm.

The work I was doing was good work, to stop some megalomaniacal plot. The work had to go on. So I sat down again.

In Australia, the front for all this evil machinery was to be Telecom, poor innocent Telecom. Somebody I knew worked there. Why didn't I ask him? No, this was confidential. I was not supposed to know anything. My translation of the German was going to France. But how could this help my dear Australia? Would France do something about it? What could I do alone in Rome? What about Britain? Could I contact someone in Britain? No, I was sworn to secrecy. My work was confidential. What a burden to bear. Yet bear it I must.

"Once the people are marked . . ."

The people must not be marked! How are the people to be saved from this fate worse than death? This wicked system to carry out wicked purposes had to be stopped. Well, we overcame them in the last war and we will overcome them again. How wise we are all going to have to be.

How are we going to save the people from being marked?

The people must keep their good currency. The system was to take away people's money. The system was to mark all food and manufactured items with a bar code. People would not be able to buy or sell food etc. without the bar code and their corresponding mark or number on their hand or forehead. A diabolical system and totally insane.

What fool would devise such a plot! What fool would fall for it! Australians weren't like that. Australians were thinking people and so were the peoples of the whole world. Hardworking people deserve something better.

The last page came.

"These are the locations for Australia . . .No. 4a Herbert Street, St. Leonards, N.S.W. 2065. . . . *und so weiter . . .* and so on."

It was done. finished.

I rang my contact. The telephone was answered immediately.

"*Merci bien, Mademoiselle. Je viens tout de suite.* — Thank you very much, Mademoiselle. I will come at once."

My hand was shaking. The envelope was sealed as arranged. All the energy seemed drained from me. In passing I looked in the mirror. It was not my face, but the face of someone I did not know, white like someone close to death.

My first thought was to drink whisky, but one thing I had learned, never drink on your own.

So, old-fashioned, I took out my smelling salts. The strong ammonia smell brought me back to my senses. Now I felt steadier.

The door bell rang. This time the courier smiled. "We are eternally grateful, Mademoiselle." The cheque was again more than we had agreed.

The money meant nothing. I wished I had never accepted the assignment. And yet my work was for a good cause, to expose an evil plot. Only good would come from its exposure, nauseating as the exposure might be.

Everyone in the Embassy was over-friendly to me in the morning.

"Is anything wrong? You don't look too well. Can we help? Why not take a day off?"

"No, thank you. It will pass. A hot cup of tea and I'll be all right."

How I enjoy my Embassy work. Tourists with major problems, lost passports, stolen luggage, missing friends, all fell into insignificance as passports, missing goods and friends were found. Insurance Companies eventually paid up for missing goods. Everything fell into place and life ran smoothly.

Then a special messenger arrived. It was not my silent courier. Was something wrong? Quickly I opened the envelope: *"Mademoiselle, the contact who has been providing our information from Germany has been murdered, stabbed to death. As our work has been discovered and we have lost our source of information, our agreement is now terminated. We are very grateful and sorry to give you such short notice. Your final cheque in payment is enclosed. Should we have a further opportunity to use your services, we shall be pleased to contact you. Our many thanks."*

Relief did not stop me from being sick. In the privacy of the washroom, tears ran down my cheeks. Someone had been killed. If we had continued, could this have been me? My nausea seemed uncontrollable, until I realised I had done good. Part of the plot had been exposed and good would come. There was nothing more to be done now.

My assignment was over.

Alex was to fly in tomorrow and life would be sweet again and I was that little bit wiser.

The sunshine in the Piazza near the Embassy was warm, and the aroma of freshly-percolated coffee refreshing as I walked out to lunch. The freshly-baked rolls smelt delicious, and the fragrance of the fresias and hyacinths in the tubs of flowers was heavenly.

As I lifted my cup and looked up into the azure blue sky, I saw a figure disappearing behind the blue door opposite. I sat very still, but there was no more movement.

What did it matter? The assignment was over.

Gorgeous Gigolo

"Sir, to take out an insurance policy on the unexpected death of your wife, a lady of seventy-six years, would cost quite a sum. Yes, the proceeds of the policy, $3 million are great, but is it worth it? Yes, I know it only covers your short overseas trip together, and I have your doctor's certificate to confirm your wife is in excellent health for her age. All right, if you are happy to accept the nominated figure, we'll go right ahead. And for yourself?"

"Oh no, I'm in excellent health. I'm only thirty-six years old and really in my prime. It is just my wife I am concerned about."

The girls behind the insurance office desk nudged each other. When the client had gone, they all broke out together. "He's just after her money. She's old enough to be his grandmother. It's disgusting! He'll bump her off and collect the insurance as well."

Raoul stepped out into the warm Brisbane sunshine smiling to himself. Anita, slim and young, the brilliant sunshine highlighting her glossy black hair, was waiting.

"Did you get it?"

He showed her the policy. "$3 million is a lot of money, and with the inheritance when she dies, our dreams will come true. Just be patient. I have to get back to her now."

Anita slipped away and Raoul went to the florist.

"Good morning, Mr Amare. The usual? You spoil your wife, you know. The fragrant luculia and pink dahlias are quite lovely at the moment, but the imported roses are very dear just now."

"No, she always likes roses. Forget the cost. Nothing is too good for my wife."

Raoul's dark eyes flashed over the florist's shapely hips, and his dimples deepened enticingly in his handsome face. He winked.

"Goodbye, Mr Amare."

Outside, Raoul took a deep breath. It was a short walk to the mansion, half of which Jean had signed over to him as part of the marriage settlement. He knew she would be waiting, waiting for him to flatter her, caress her, charm her. The thought of her wrinkles made him shudder. But then he thought of appetizing Anita and the future, and he strode on gaining confidence and determination with every step.

At the gate a familiar figure stepped out from the bushes. "It's time, Raoul."

"Oh, give us a break, Eddy. You know it's not time. April, next month, I told you, you'll be paid in full. You know the situation."

"I thought I'd just inform you. I'll be there on April the 16th to collect. The syndicate has got a job for me in Biarritz, a jewellery job. But in the meantime, I need something now. I'll wait here for you."

Raoul clenched the roses tightly. So much depended on him. But it was worth it. He walked up the drive.

"Darling!" Jean's blonded head appeared at the window.

As he entered the front door he heard her high heels tapping down the spiral staircase.

"Dearest" he whispered, giving her the usual lovebite she so liked behind her ear.

She squealed with delight. "Look at my new peignoir. I bought it for the trip. How do you like it?" She swirled around, tripping on her too high heel, and letting him catch her in his arms.

"Oh, Raoul. You look so handsome today." Her hands caressed his upper arms, sensing the power in his muscles. "To bed, Raoul. Come to bed."

His muscles flexed involuntarily and his set smile hid his distaste. Outwardly he oozed all charm.

"Dearest!" He kissed her again gently under the ear and then they walked up the stairs their arms around each other.

After it was over, Jean lay back euphoric. "Leave me now, Raoul. Just the roses. Leave me the roses. Here, you'll need this." She reached into her gleaming leather purse and handed him a bundle of $100 notes. "You do it so well, darling. I'll see you tonight."

He bowed. Still he remembered his training, respect at all times. Then he backed out the door.

At the gate, Eddy took $300. "Next time we'll meet in Biarritz. So long!"

All the preparations for the flight had been made. Jean was nervously hanging on to his arm. "You know, my first husband always travelled overseas alone, he always left me at home. Of course it was always business. That's where he made all his money, overseas. Our money, now, darling." She squeezed his arm possessively.

Raoul had learnt to keep a continuous smile on his face. "So handsome" as Jean kept saying. "My gorgeous husband." Her girlfriend, Maisie, had always accused her of using Raoul as her gorgeous gigolo, but she did not object. It gave her power. Power to have Raoul just the way she wanted him, and she was not going to surrender that power. She squeezed her purse tightly and smiled at the air hostess as she settled her comfortably in her seat. "Thank you, dear" she pressed the $20 note into the hostess's hand, assured of receiving all the attention she needed on the trip.

Raoul's eyes met the hostess's and a smile flickered between them.

"You know I am thinking of changing my Will again Raoul" her voice interrupted his dreams.

He sat up bolt upright.

"Yes. Of course, you still receive the bulk of the estate but I've been thinking lately of the little children being orphaned in that terrible war in the Balkans. Every time I watch it on television my heart bleeds. I've just sent off a cheque for $5,000 and I'm leaving a provision also in my Will."

Raoul interrupted. "$5,000! Do you think that's wise? We'll need that."

"Oh no, Raoul. I've told you how much my husband left in the estate and the investments are bringing in thousands a week. $5,000 is nothing. Next month I may make it $10,000."

Raoul swallowed hard. "Well, let's not be hasty. This is our honeymoon you know. You don't want to think business on a honeymoon. Wait till we get back."

She smiled dreamily.

The hotel was right on the beach. It was their third day, April the 15th and the Spring sunshine lit up the tubs of fragrant fresias and vibrant bougainvillea.

Jean thought she recognized that girl, Anita, who was always hanging around Raoul. What was she doing here? Jean frowned thoughtfully.

After dinner Raoul pretended not to see Eddy, flitting among the bejewelled ladies in the foyer. Eddy made a victory sign with his fingers and whispered "tomorrow" as he sauntered by.

The dance started up. "Let's dance, darling. Let's dance the night away."

Raoul felt a headache coming on. "Couldn't we retire early tonight?"

"You look strained, dear. All those travel arrangements. You've done them so well. Yes, let's go to bed." She squeezed his arm invitingly.

Their backs, seen going up the spacious staircase together, looked more like a protective grandmother and her wayward grandson kept well in tow.

It was 6 o'clock in the morning when a terrified Mrs Amare telephoned the desk and called for an ambulance. "Send the doctor, quickly. My husband . . ." her voice gasped.

When the doctor arrived, he found a distraught dowager gasping for breath. Before proceeding further, he sat her down and gave her a sedative. He felt her pulse. It was racing. "Now what is the matter, my dear?"

She could not speak but kept gasping, pointing to the bathroom. He heard her sobbing on the lounge as he opened the door.

In the bath was the body of a man, a young man of fine physique, yet bloated by immersion in quite cold water.

"I am so sorry, my dear. When did this happen?"

Jean gripped her handkerchief tightly. "Last night. Last

night he gave me my medicine and went to take a bath. I must have had too large a dose because I became drowsy and must have fallen asleep. When I woke up this morning, I realized he hadn't slept with me. I don't know what had come over me. I just passed out last night and then, and then when I got up, and I'm still feeling a bit dizzy, I went into the bathroom and . . ." She broke out into uncontrollable sobs.

"My dear, this is a terrible shock for you. Will you let me send a nurse to take you to a private hospital where you can have rest. It takes several days to recover from this kind of shock."

Jean nodded like a little child.

"In the meantime . . ." the doctor telephoned for the police and the hotel manager.

"Mais, c'est impossible! C'est horrible!" The hotel manager was beside himself. "We've never had anything like this before. Our reputation! *Pardonnez moi, Madame.*"

Inspector Murdoch from the FBI appeared on the scene. He had been called to the hotel following a number of jewel thefts the night before. "I don't suppose this is linked with the others?" he mused. "My condolences, Mrs Amare. Could you please tell me what happened?"

Jean rubbed her hand over her forehead. "I'm not thinking very clearly. I think I must have had too much of my medicine. Really, I just went to bed and then I woke up this morning and it was all over. Raoul! Raoul!" She sobbed uncontrollably.

"The medicine bottle?"

She pointed to the bedroom. The bottle was there on the bedside table.

"It smells all right. A bit like garlic. I'll have it analysed."

The nurse arrived and helped Mrs Amare to the ambulance.

The inspector was discussing the case with several of the local police officers, when the door was suddenly pushed open. A confident Eddy froze as he stared at the police officers. His mouth fell open, but then he quickly became mobile, turned and raced out the door towards the stairs.

"After him, Sergeant!" The chief inspector barked and Eddy was apprehended half-way down.

"Take him to lock up! We'll question him later."
"I didn't do it! I didn't do it!"
Eddy was taken out through the hotel lobby.
"Now then, Doctor, what is the verdict?"
"Well, it doesn't make sense. He's a young man, healthy it would seem. But he's died of a massive heart attack. The body's been in the water for about eight hours. We'll need an autopsy."
"Not just drowning? Suicide perhaps?"
"No. There are symptoms of a massive shock! Very strange. Very strange indeed."
"No marks, finger marks pressed on the body, bruises, bleeding?"
"Nothing at all."
"We'll take the body away and see what Forensic have to say."
A young police office appeared at the door. "There's been another incident in the foyer. A young woman, Anita Kellerman, with an Australian passport, became hysterical and they're calming her down in the manager's office."
Murdoch strode downstairs, his six feet towering over the milling crowd whispering in the foyer and noting each new event with avid curiosity.
"In here, Inspector."
"Anita, is it? Anita Kellerman?"
Anita was still sipping a glass of water. Her face had drained deathly white.
"Here, dear" the elderly office assistant handed her a small phial of smelling salts.
She sniffed and her head seemed to clear. "I don't understand." She burst into sobs. "I saw Mrs Amare being taken out to the ambulance and then I was told Raoul was dead." She could not speak but rocked backwards and forwards.
"You knew the deceased?"
"Yes. He was a friend."
"And what are you doing here in Biarritz?"
"A holiday. It was just a coincidence that Raoul, Raoul and his wife were staying here."
Murdoch studied her intently. "Just a coincidence?"

"Yes" her voice was just a whisper. "I think I'll go back to my room now."

The doctor came walking through the lobby on his way out.

"Any more thoughts, Doctor? Could he have been put in the bath after death? A strong man like Eddy could have done it. And then come back to the scene of the crime."

"I don't know really. I'd be very interested in the forensic report. Must get back to the practice now. Let me know Inspector. Good hunting!"

Inspector Murdoch returned to the room. Luxury and affluence was all around, clothing, jewellery, luggage, everything was expensive. There was an insurance policy listing all their personal effects, covered for a handsome sum. Inspector Murdoch whistled. "What's this? A policy on Mrs Amare in case of unexpected death!" He searched. "But nothing on him. That's odd. Who benefits from his death, I wonder?" He walked slowly from the room.

It took some time to contact their solicitor in Australia. Mrs Amare had only just remarried. Her first husband, a business tycoon had died just eighteen months before, leaving her a multi-millionairess. There were no children and no relatives, other than the husband it seemed. She had been in the habit of writing large cheques to charities. Her last Will was made out exclusively with her husband as beneficiary.

"And his Will?" Murdoch asked.

"Well, he didn't leave his Will with me. There was a lot of mystery about that. I handled most of their legal work. She handled all the finances, quite large cheques made out to him regularly. If he didn't leave a Will, his estate would go to her automatically, but it wouldn't amount to much, I shouldn't think."

Murdoch was thoughtful. It was a pity Mrs Amare had blacked out. She was the last to see her husband alive.

He went back to the hotel room. There were no signs of 'break-in and steal'. Baffling. Funny about that garlic smell in her medicine. That was the first clue he'd follow up.

The laboratory report was quite clear. There was arsenic in the medicine prescription. They had contacted her doctor in Australia and there was no problem about that. But in the present bottle there was an excessive quantity of arsenic, a fatal dose, in fact enough to cause death six times over.

"And yet she only slept for, what? Eight hours. She blacked out, in fact more or less when he took his heart attack, about 10 p.m. Could someone have tried to kill her and then murdered him? The time factor is very interesting. Was there anyone else there? I must ask her."

Jean Amare was looking very drawn, not a pretty sight with blonded hair dry and sticking up around her face. 'An odd marriage,' crossed Inspector Murdoch's mind. He moved up and sat on her bed. "Well, how are you feeling this morning, Mrs Amare?"

She looked like death warmed up. "I've been thinking Inspector, about that medicine last night. Raoul always gives it to me and we make love for at least half an hour before it takes effect, and then I have a beautiful sleep. But last night, being our honeymoon, I didn't feel like taking medicine, so I only pretended to. When Raoul turned to take his bath, I spat most of it out into my handkerchief. I didn't want him to know, so I flushed the handkerchief down the toilet. When I got back into bed, well, I just passed out. I don't know what Raoul did. We didn't make love. I don't remember anything."

"Was there anyone else in your room that night?"

"No, no-one. We were really on our honeymoon, you know." Mrs Amare started to weep.

"And did your husband in fact go straight to the bathroom and take a bath?"

"Well, I heard him go in. I heard the bath running. I don't know what happened after that." She was sobbing and confused.

Inspector Murdoch left the hospital with the memory of her face drained of all life.

When he returned to headquarters, the laboratory report had been put on his desk. Who had put the extra arsenic in the medicine? If it was the husband, we'll never know. Fingerprints? Fingerprints had been wiped off. Had Mrs Amare done that with her handkerchief? He should have asked her. She'd said there was nobody in the room at the time of the murder, but then she'd blacked out almost immediately. Had somebody else come in? Eddy looked as though he knew something. Why had he walked so confidently in? What did he expect to find?

Eddy was in the police cell refusing to talk. Nothing had been found on him. "I've done nothing" he kept saying.

"What were you doing at the Amare's hotel?"

"I came to see Raoul. We're friends. We both came over from Australia. I just called in to see him."

"At 7 o'clock in the morning?"

"Yeah. Well, he'd told me to call on him first thing. So that's what I did."

"And why did you run away when you saw the police officers there?"

"Well, I didn't know what was going on. I didn't see Raoul. I thought I must be in the wrong room, so I left."

"What do you know about Raoul's death?"

"Nothing. I don't know nothing. You can't pin that on me."

"What are you doing in Biarritz?"

"Holiday. Just a holiday."

"How can you afford it? What's your profession?"

"I'm a . . . a . . . I'm an investor."

"Oh yes, what do you invest in?"

"Well, I win most of me money on the races. I've been lucky just lately. Thought I'd enjoy a holiday. Biarritz. A nice place."

"On your own?"

"Yeah."

"Your address?"

"Well, I don't have an address at the moment."

"How's that?"

"I was kicked out of the room where I was staying. Then I got lost. Can't remember where it was. These French names, they get me. I can't remember."

"We'll find out. In the meantime, this'll be your address for a while."

"On what grounds?"

"Suspicious behaviour, unlicensed entering of premises, suspect at the scene of a murder . . ."

"Hey, wait on. Raoul's my friend. I want to find out just

as much as you do."

"Last night there were some jewels stolen from guests' rooms in the hotel. Do you know anything about that?"

A quick flicker of concern lit up his eye. "Jewellery. I don't know about no jewellery. Holiday, that's what I'm here for, a holiday and you're b . . . well turning it into a nightmare."

"Until you can give us an address, enjoy your cell here."

Murdoch went back to the office. Along with all the other questions, he kept asking himself, "Who benefited from Raoul's death?"

As if in answer to his question, he received a phone call from a prominent Biarritz solicitor. "Have just read in the newspaper that my client, Mrs Jean Amare has been taken to a private hospital. I wonder if you'd mind giving me her address."

"Your client?"

"Yes, she came to me the day after her arrival here and had her Will changed."

"Oh yes."

"She was very concerned to leave an ongoing legacy to the children left war victims. So we have arranged this with a proviso, should the husband predecease her, the whole proceeds were to be given and invested for these unfortunate victims."

"I see. Would you mind if we went to see her now together? She's not a young woman, and is all alone in a strange city."

Two hours later they were asking at the desk to see Mrs Amare.

"Haven't you heard? Of course not. They couldn't locate you. I'm sorry but Mrs Amare died one hour ago. I'll call the doctor to speak to you."

Inspector Murdoch and the solicitor shook their heads. "What bad luck! First him, now her. Ah, Doctor!"

"Come into my office, gentlemen. Yes, it's very unfortunate. She just slipped away. Natural causes. It's rather a case of delayed shock. It has all been too much for her. She has no-one here to be with her and comfort her, and her heart just failed. Totally unexpected. She was on sedatives of course, but she just could not take it. Rather an unfortunate episode altogether."

"Yes indeed." The two men took their leave.

When Inspector Murdoch arrived back at headquarters the phone was ringing.

"A break through on the jewellery robbery."

"Yes?"

"Eddy did it. We checked out his address and the jewels were there all right."

"Thanks. I think I'll go and have another chat with him."

"Well, Eddy, your sins have found you out. One problem solved. Now, what about the murder?"

"I didn't do it. I never done the murder. Look, I'll tell you. Raoul owed me money, or rather owed the boss. Raoul told me the 16th April he was going to come into a lot of money. He'd have his hands on millions, with millions more to come, so the boss lent him a couple of grand to pay his debts. I went there that morning to collect my stake. When I arrived, well you know the rest. When I saw the cops I thought they were after me for the robberies. I ran, that's all, I ran."

Inspector Murdoch went back to the hotel. The room was still cordoned off, nothing had been touched. He walked around the room musing.

Had nothing been touched? He picked up the insurance inventory — suitcases, jewellery, clothing, personal belongings, shaver. He went into the bathroom, the shaver was still there. Lady's hair dryer. He looked around, in the drawers, cupboards. No lady's hair dryer. He called his offsider on duty downstairs. "Here. Help check this out. There's a lady's hair dryer listed here. I can't find it."

Together they searched. No lady's hair dryer. He even looked in the wastepaper basket. It was empty but the floral patterned material around it was wet.

Inspector Murdoch's little grey cells started to come to life. He walked into the bathroom.

What if Mrs Amare was suspicious that her husband had tried to poison her? In self-defence she goes into the bathroom where her husband is taking a bath. She plugs her hair dryer into the power point, switches it on and throws it into the bath. He is electrocuted immediately, exhibiting the symptoms of a violent heart attack. She carefully switches it off and unplugs it. Then she pushes him under the water to make it look like drowning. She puts the wet hair drier in the wastepaper basket.

Yes, but where is it now?

Let's ask the night cleaners.

Yes, the night cleaners were going down the corridor and saw the hair dryer put out in the wastepaper basket, so they took it. Probably Mrs Amare brought in the empty basket herself and put it back in its place.

After the murder, Mrs Amare pretended to be drugged until the morning, acting innocent of the fact that her husband lay dead in the bath, hoping it would be assumed he had drowned. Maybe she died of remorse.

So, who wins out of all this?

Ah yes, the little children orphaned in the war.

How true. "All things work for good . . . . ."

Death by Slow Deprivation

The wedding guests threw handfuls of fragrant rose petals over the bride outside the church, as organ strains of "Oh Perfect Love" floated on the cool evening air. Surprisingly all the guests were neighbours and friends, as neither the bride nor the groom had any living relatives. "A love match not marred by interfering in-laws" said one of the neighbours. "What a happy pair!"

The cameras clicked as the bride, now Mrs Desmond Smith, smiled, looking radiant, as the setting sun shone on her soft blonde hair lightly waved under the demure veil, her innocent blue eyes matching the azure cloudless sky above.

Bronwyn Betteridge, the well-known mystery writer, was riding past the church on her mountain bicycle and stopped to comment to her friend Betty Mitchell "Oh what a lovely bride! I hope they'll be very happy!"

"Well, I don't know" said Betty. "I've known Veronica for a long time. She and her former husband Les lived here in Bullaburra, making the Blue Mountains their home, for fifteen years. Les was much older than her of course, but he adored her. And then one day, quite suddenly, he suffered a coronary, not unusual of course for a man in his seventies. We all knew he was too old for her but it was a love match. Veronica's only forty now. His death was such a loss. He left her his huge home and made sure she was quite well off, and she's been managing very well on her own up till now. This wedding is too soon. She hasn't had time to cope with her grief properly yet. This younger man, what do we know of him?"

"He's very handsome" commented Bronwyn noting his tall, strong frame, dark well-groomed hair, dark eyes and well-tailored wedding suit.

"Handsome is as handsome does" observed Betty thoughtfully.

"What does he do for a living?"

"That's just it. He's not working at the moment. Says it's the recession. They met doing a course on Economics Management."

"Oh, he'll make good" said Bronwyn, mounting her bicycle.

"I hope so" said Betty waving goodbye.

The Reception was a modest, happy affair at the Grand View. The log fires were burning warmly and the wedding supper served in the cosy glow. Desmond clung to his wife and would not let her out of his sight. They danced beautifully together and he barely let her go as she went up to the bridal room to change. When she reappeared at the top of the staircase, she looked lovely in pink silk suit and feathered toque, she had chosen for her going-away outfit.

"She looks like a gossamer butterfly" one of the guests commented.

Desmond came forward to take her hand. His eyes focussed on the glittering Oroton handbag with a cluster of deep red roses.

Their first night was at Felton Woods, before proceeding next day to the Jenolan Caves for their honeymoon.

"Here, baby-eyes, you pay for the cab. I don't want to change a $100 note. I'll take the cases in."

Veronica was taken aback. "Where was the attentive fiancé she had married?" she wondered as she stared at the back of her husband, disappearing through the glass doors.

"Thank you. You're a real lady" the driver smiled as she gave him a handsome tip.

When they were alone in their suite, Veronica turned to Desmond. "Why did you leave me to pay for the cab?" she asked.

"Oh, Veronica, don't be so petty. It was just a cab fare. Come on!" He grabbed her and threw her onto the bed. "This's what marriage is all about."

His lovemaking wasn't enjoyable. Desmond was hard and cruel. "No gain without pain" he kept saying.

When it was over, he was pleased with himself. "I'm just going out for a walk. Have the unpacking done when I get back." He whistled jauntily as he stepped out the door.

Veronica lay exhausted on the bed, bruised and confused. "What had come over Desmond? No longer was he the caring, solicitous man who had courted her, but an ugly brute." Quietly she went over to make a cup of tea, puzzling all the time. The element of the jug had blown so she took her handbag and went downstairs to the coffee lounge.

An elderly lady was sitting on her own.

"Do you mind if I join you?"

"No, please do."

They had a good chat and then Desmond came rushing through the door. "What are you doing here?"

"What do you mean, what am I doing here? I'm having a coffee."

"Oh no, you don't." He grabbed her possessively by the arm and hauled her from the seat.

The older woman looked dismayed.

Veronica smiled weakly and said "Good night. I may see you in the morning."

Desmond squeezed her elbow tightly, painfully. "Oh no you won't. You're married to me and you do what I want from now on."

Once again when they reached their suite, it was a sudden toss on the bed and bully tactics all over again. Then Desmond snatched her purse. "How much have you been spending while I was out?" He held her bag possessively. "I'll take this. If you want any money, you can ask me."

The gentle evening breeze was lost on Veronica's sobs of shock and concern. "What was going on?"

The honeymoon was over. Life began to settle down in their spacious home at the end of their quiet street next to the thick bushland.

Veronica never saw her neighbours now. Previously she had been very concerned for the Sherbrook family of six who had lost all their savings in a Building Society collapse. It

Slowly her fighting spirit had been crushed and more often than not she found herself in tears. Her will, her spirit, were slowly being eroded. Physically Desmond towered over her. There seemed no way to communicate with him. She had demanded to see a doctor when his bruising became violent bleeding, but he insisted she stay silent or he would do worse.

As the days passed she found she could not eat. Mentally she was worried sick trying to fathom it out. What was she doing wrong? What should she do? Who was this monster gnawing at her, strangling her every emotion, and what for? Money? Well, if that was the case, he might as well have it and let her go. But he would not let her go. Freedom seemed an elusive term fading into the distance.

Then one day, Desmond decided they would move back home.

Veronica went out into the garden and picked clumps of garlic. She had heard that slivers of garlic between the toes enabled the juices to be absorbed and carried up into the body. It was sure way to keep healthy. For the first time Desmond left her alone. It was heaven. She lay on the bed peacefully and had her first night's sleep. Slowly she began to feel better.

Desmond still threatened her occasionally, clasping the pointed serrated knife kept by the kitchen bench. She kept telling herself that her worries were nothing compared to others. Her heart was torn by the families destitute in the Recession and she felt better after sending a substantial cheque. When she went to do the same again, she found her chequebook, bank books and financial statements, along with her documents and credit cards were no longer in her attaché case. What was Desmond up to?

It was late Autumn afternoon. The wind was sending a flurry of fallen Autumn leaves rustling along the gutters, golds, reds and crackling brown leaves. Desmond left the house with his jacket pulled tight around him and began to walk. He was in no hurry. He had made an appointment with the local doctor for 4.30 p.m., and he wanted to be seen around the shopping centre, doing the usual household shopping.

Dr Meredith was a quietly spoken man. "How may I help

you, Mr Smith?''

"Well, it's my wife, Doctor. She's been acting strangely lately. I've been trying to talk her into making a visit but she won't come. Really I was wondering if you could possibly make a house call.''

"What are her symptoms?''

"She has severe depression, won't leave the house, leaves all the shopping and so on to me. She has a fear of talking to people, and just locks herself inside all day.''

"How long has this been going on for?''

"Nearly three months now.''

"Why didn't you come to see me about it earlier?''

"Well, I just kept hoping she'd snap out of it. It's just now she's been talking of committing suicide and it's worrying me.''

"All right, I have just one more patient to see and then I'll come with you and call on her.''

It was after 5 p.m. when the doctor closed his surgery. A chill wind had set in when they drove up to the front door.

"It's me dear'' Desmond called, unlocking the front door. "She always likes me to reassure her.''

"Gas! What's that terrible smell of gas?'' The doctor sniffed and grew tense.

"It's coming from the kitchen. This way!''

When they opened the door, the smell was overpowering. The doctor held a handkerchief over is nose, raced to the oven and switched off the gas. He pointed to Desmond to open all the windows.

The gas was asphyxiating but the doctor went straight to the woman whose body was comfortably relaxed on a chair, her head resting on a tea towel inside the oven door. He carried her out gently onto the verandah.

"She's been dead some time'' he said. "When did you leave her?''

"It was about 3 o'clock. I left to do some shopping and came on to you for my appointment at 4.30.''

"And she was all right when you left her?''

"Yes, perfectly. Except . . . well, she said again: 'I'm going to end it' but she's been saying that a lot over the last few months. That's why I came to see you. I gave her a cup of tea and promised to be back soon. That was the last I saw her alive." Desmond broke out in dry racking sobs.

"Looks like you'd better make yourself a cup of tea. Take this sedative. It's a nasty shock. I'll call the police and have the ambulance take the body away."

"I'll go and call them. We're not on the phone."

"No need" said Dr Meredith, "I've got my mobile phone with me."

Shortly after, Inspector Murdoch arrived with the forensic team. "This is a tragedy" was his first comment. "She must have been a good-looking woman. She didn't leave a suicide note?" he asked.

"No, nothing." Desmond looked dazed.

Soon after, the body was taken away.

Desmond decided to spend the night at a nearby hotel. There was nothing more to be done.

Bronwyn Betteridge heard the news from a friend of hers, a nurse at the hospital. "What do you know?" the nurse added. "There was no gas found in the lungs!"

"I knew it," Bronwyn exclaimed. "He's killed her. But how do we prove it? He's done it, I know he has."

Bronwyn Betteridge stood talking to Inspector Murdoch. "You know and I know that he did it, but how do we prove it and convict him? For the moment he's perfectly free. Suicide they say."

"Criminals usually give some little clue themselves. They are so conceited at carrying out their crime, they want somebody to know how clever they've been. In the meantime, they often go off and repeat the crime, unfortunately."

"I'm trying to find out more on his background. It could be he has a history of this?" suggested Bronwyn.

"Good idea. In the meanwhile, we'll keep him watched."

For the first couple of days the police officers on watch in unmarked cars were beginning to think their efforts futile, but on the fifth night, Desmond emerged with a suitcase which he put in the boot and drove away. Unfortunately at a railway crossing they lost him.

Bronwyn's investigation of 'Missing Persons' revealed a

Mr Derek Smythe missing for about six months before his wedding to Veronica. He had been in a penal institution on charges of rape and child abuse, and then was transferred to a rehabilitation hospital on his plea of diminished responsibility.

Bronwyn discussed her findings with Inspector Murdoch. "He got out chatting up one of the nurses, convinced her he shouldn't be there and walked out with her as her date. He is described as a handsome, powerful man. As soon as they were outside the gates, he pushed her behind the trees, smashed her face, raped her, took her handbag and then stabbed her, leaving her half-dead and bleeding profusely. The nurse was found by a police patrol and taken back inside the hospital. She was able to tell them that Derek did it, just before she died. The alert has been out on him ever since, but no sign of him. There have been a few leads, it seems he's changed his name a number of times. From the description, it looks as though Derek Smythe and Desmond Smith are one and the same man."

"If that's the case, we'll have to bring him in. There's no knowing what he'll do next."

"I have a terrible feeling about this" Bronwyn urged Inspector Murdoch. "Do you think we could have the gas cut off at the home? We don't want anything like that happening again."

"Yes, no reason why not. He's left the place for the moment, but we're keeping a watch on the house. Unfortunately the men tailing his car lost him. I'm sure he'll be back."

It was only three days later when the police watching the house were alerted that Desmond's car was returning. They kept well out of sight.

Desmond stopped the car. He put his arm around a blonde woman who had been sitting on the seat next to him and together, laughing, they took two cases from the boot and made their way into the house.

"Watch this one" Inspector Murdoch urged his men. "We don't want another accident."

They had barely entered the house, when a scream came

from the kitchen.

"Right men, this is it!" The police forced their way in.

The woman was being held forcibly by Desmond, using all his strength to force her head well into the oven, only this time nothing was happening.

"What's wrong?" he asked holding her tightly.

"The gas has been turned off," Inspector Murdoch advised.

"He tried to kill me! He tried to kill me!" the woman screamed hysterically. "He's a madman."

"Gas in the lungs. Just going to prove, gas in the lungs." Desmond looked dazed and disoriented. He mumbled to himself, "Nobody saw me smother Veronica with that pillow. She gassed herself. That's how it was."

"He's got my handbag!" The woman suddenly came to life. "That's what he was after."

"He's responsible for a lot more than that." Murdoch turned to Desmond. "Your wife was a beautiful and gentle woman. It's a pity you never learnt to value her."

"Oh no, treat 'em rough. I learnt that in the institution."

"What institution?"

Desmond was suddenly silent. "You're not going to put me back there." He reached out for the pointed knife on the kitchen bench.

Five police revolvers pointed at him.

His eyes spun crazily. With a sudden movement he drove the knife forcefully into his throat, choking and coughing blood as the jugular vein severed.

The woman screamed and was led out by one of the police officers.

"He got what was coming to him. He was incapable of remorse. Things will go back to normal now." Inspector Murdoch looked at the motionless body.

Bronwyn Betteridge turned from the ugly sight. It's surprising he's been out living a normal life for so long."

"Oh well, the law's like that these days. Criminals and others are released onto the society to cope with as best we can. Thank goodness this chapter is closed. I'm sorry about his wife."

"The only good thing, her wish will be carried out. She

wanted her home to be given to the Sherbrook family, and now this will be done. She confided in me some time ago."

Bronwyn Betteridge pedalled thoughtfully back to her home. Maybe women in the United States were right to arm themselves these days? It would not hurt to have a bit of 4 × 2 by the door just in case. No defence like self-defence. She'd stay home more often now and keep an eye out for her neighbours too. In the meantime she'd bake a cake, a nice honey cake for the Sherbrooks. It will be good to have a happy family living in 'Silver Chimes'. Veronica would be pleased.

One Woman's War

History repeats itself. Archduke Francis Ferdinand, heir to the Austro-Hungarian throne was assassinated in Sarajevo, capital of the annexed territory of Bosnia-Herzegovina. Austria gave an ultimatum to Serbia. So started World War I.

In December 1991, Germany, followed by the European Community, recognized Croatia and Slovenia as Independent States against Yugoslavia. In the words of one Serbian soldier on 8th December 1991, "This is war with fascism in Croatia, the Germans and Austrians are on their side. There are Fascists in Australia and the USA." Sarajevo again is the site of initial "ethnic cleansing" with families and homes being decimated and bus loads of their children taken to East Germany.

It is strange how 'Peace' can mean 'War'. On 23rd February 1992, the then German Foreign Minister, Hans Dietrich Genscher, visited Croatia with 14,000 peacekeeping force available and urged the acceptance of the United Nations' peace plan. Since then there has been nothing but escalating war.

In Australia, Prime Minister Keating and his wife, were encouraging ties with Germany and keen to see Australia a Republic. On 18th June 1992 he passed legislation to turn Australia into a world nuclear dump. All power was given to ANSTO, Australian Nuclear Science Technology Organisation excluding it from State Environmental Laws.

An agreement has been made between the European

Community and Australia on patents and trademarks. A university for Australian studies has been set up in Pottsdam and Brandenburg, East Germany so Germany can study Australia's ecology, climatic research, mining and recultivation.

When five years after Black Tuesday, 20th October 1987, the world Stock Market crash, on Black Wednesday, 16th September 1992, the £Sterling fell below the accepted level of the ERM, Exchange Rate Mechanism. Germany who was raking in all the money at very high interest rates, said to Britain "You look after your own back yard". So much for European community.

So, One Woman's War began.

"You take your own advice, Germany, you look after your own back yard and I'll look after mine." It has put me on the defensive.

The ugly head of Fascism, Dictatorship, Inflation, reveals this to be very much an Economic War.

Step No. 1 was to evacuate the city, leave Sydney the beautiful city on the harbour, my birthplace with so many happy memories and move to the country. Continuing to work in the city, meant travelling seven hours a day, five days a week, leaving home in subzero temperatures in winter, never seeing the garden in daylight until the weekends. This enabled me to pay for my home, which I had purchased in fact some years earlier.

Coming from the city, the first thing that confronted me as unusual was a venomous black snake curled up on the path. When it saw me coming with the hose, it slowly slithered between the air vents under the house and disappeared under my bedroom.

Snakes are protected, so I telephoned the National Parks and Wildlife Office. They gave me the number of the local snake-catcher.

"Hello! No, m'son's not home. This is his dad. You've got a black snake have you. Well the red bellies are the females. I've got nine of them. Don't worry, the cat'll catch it. Goodbye."

If this is what country people do, live with their snakes, right, I'll do that.

For one week I slept with that snake under my bedroom

and visions of it coming up through the floor and landing on my bed.

The next Saturday morning, I had the urge to go round the path to that spot again. No! No way! That's where the snake is. The urge grew stronger, so I took my secateurs and nonchalantly pruned the abelia grandiflora hedge growing there, as though I hadn't a care in the world. No sooner had I started clipping, when I looked down and saw something on the path. It was a small piece of black snake, head and tail chewed off, and there in the bushes was a wild tabby cat grinning his whiskers off!

"You darling!" I exclaimed and he beamed all the more. So I there and then named him "Oscar" for his award-winning performance. Then I tried to tame him. He was completely wild and when I offered him some delicious food, he spat, scratched, purred and hissed all at the same time, he didn't know what to do. But he was happy. Little by little we became friends and eventually he rolled on his back on the patio in the sun while I stroked his soft belly. He had an excellent coat for the cold Blue Mountains' winter, tabby on the outside and very thick soft fur close to his skin.

Oscar was Nature's offspring indeed. Although he was not desexed, he was the nicest cat I shall ever know. Oscar was a Recession cat. He had two homes and knew which side his bread was buttered. When he was well fed and plump, he would leave me for about six months. It always happened when I was feeling the pinch, Oscar would appear at the door thin and starving. I was overjoyed and immediately filled the house with food and fattened Oscar up again once more.

One day a dog fought Oscar, and although he won the battle, he had a tooth infection, so I bundled him up in the cat basket and took him to the vet. Would he insist he be desexed? No.

"Oscar" the vet said, "is older than we think. He has had a tough battle in life out there. His kidneys have failed and a blood test showed he will not last more than a week." He fixed up his mouth infection and advised he would have to be put down.

'No,' I thought. 'I'll take Oscar home with me to die in peace.'

The vet gave him an injection to make him eat, advising

that these injections were needed each week, but Oscar would not be with us next week. He advised me to give him lots of water for his kidney failure. The vet kindly dropped us off at home on his way to visit a sick horse.

At home, I sat Oscar up on a soft rug and fed him little delicacies and waited. Each morning I came out expecting to find him lying at peace.

Two and a half years later, Oscar, hale and hearty, disappeared one night in a snowstorm. When he arrived back a few nights later, I realized that somebody had had him desexed. He was much more placid and came to sleep on the end of my bed at night. It reminded me of Sir Winston Churchill's praise for his black cat Nelson who played his part in war economy by serving as the prime ministerial hot water bottle.

Oscar continued to be no trouble, never was there an accident in the house, although he kept drinking lots of water.

Once again, tragedy struck, and Oscar came home with his stomach and back legs as though they had been gripped in a dog's mouth. He looked triumphant, but was unable to eat. This distressed me very much so I bought him some king prawns, which he managed to eat, and then while I was summing up courage to take him to the vet, he disappeared.

Three days later my neighbour came to me in tears and asked if I had seen Oscar.

"No" I said, "I think he has gone away."

"I'm sorry to tell you, a tabby cat has been found up in the bush near my neighbour's. We think it was Oscar."

Right to the end, Oscar lived a fully natural life, and this is my little tribute to him.

Continuing to look after my own back yard, I decided to keep 'chooks'. Once again I was reminded of Sir Winston Churchill "blood, toil, tears and sweat". So they could free-range, I had to put up a six foot high dogwire fence around the garden, making sure the wire was bent facing outwards under the ground, so an invading fox would scratch its paws if it tried to dig under the fence.

The rooster, Pierre, and four hens Henrietta, Charlotte,

Amelia and Emma, are a delight and live in a forest-green henhouse called *'Le Coq d'Or'*. The vegetable patch has to be protected by chicken wire. Often it is blood, toil, tears and sweat, as I defend myself from the rooster who comes flying at me assuring me this is his domain. We are still having arguments about this, my warning him "not to bite the hand that feeds him" and he crowing with great vigour about his territorial rights. My best weapon seems to be the hose turned full on in his face. Pierre has proved that you can have your cake and eat it. Cock of the roost today and also an excellent feather duster made from the many feathers moulted this Autumn.

Fowls are a very rewarding link in the Natural cycle. The fowls eat the snails and shells, and poultry manure is very beneficial around the lemon tree, on the lawns and gardens.

Fowls sometimes change their laying habits and for one week I could not find their eggs anywhere until I noticed a hen clucking as she came out from a lovely clump of agapanthos, and in the centre was a nest of eggs. Now I keep a couple of plastic eggs there to encourage the hens to lay after I remove the fresh eggs.

The constant vigilance against bush rats and mice, means practising a virtual "scorched earth policy", leave no food around. It takes great courage to set traps, melted cheese, or better still stringy salami, so the creatures are caught cleanly and neatly. Once again in the cycle of Nature, they are food for the kookaburras who swoop within half an hour of their being thrown on the roof. Not only the kookaburras but all the vibrant red and green king parrots, blue and red rosellas, silky bower birds and others make this Nature's Paradise.

Continuing to take Germany's advice, I am not only looking after my own back yard, but the front garden and Nature strip too. This produces lots of dandelions, the yellow flowers make a nourishing wine, the leaves can be tossed in salads and the roots are most beneficial, carefully washed, dried, roasted, ground and percolated into delicious coffee — excellent for liver, digestion and blood — a good cure for anaemia. The lion's tooth, jagged edged leaf, dent-de-lion, not the smooth cat's ear, must be used.

While housing is cheaper in the country, food tends to be

dearer, so shopping needs care. Transport, two hours to the city, can be expensive, but now I find I am happier staying at home. Telephoning family and friends STD has been replaced by much cheaper letter writing. Certainly in winter heating is a necessity, especially as the sun sets around 4 p.m. and a chill comes up through the ground. Drawing the curtains, putting on classical music, having a nice pot of Scotch broth bubbling and a bright log fire crackling merrily, turns night into a whole new world. While small radiators are most economical, the slow-combustion heater, which also warms food, is the most practical, and guests love the charm of wood burning, especially when we all take part in collecting the fallen branches and twigs from the pin oaks and other trees in Autumn.

Recycling becomes a way of life. The big bin has been used for rainwater, filling to the brim, and currawongs coming to drink and sing. During the short periods of no rainfall when mosquitoes tried to breed, a few drops of kerosene kept the water clear. Newspapers are used for no-dig gardens, bottles and jars for preserves, jams, chutneys and sauces. Eyes from the potatoes go into the garden, now a sizeable potato patch beside beds of garlic — the miracle cure for everything. There are twenty different herbs flourishing, their fresh fragrance highlighting *haute cuisine* along with strawberries and fruit trees. It is wonderful to propogate for family and friends.

Going back to basics, Uncle Toby's oats and Scotch broth with lamb, barley and vegetables, are excellent for the winter. Cooking, gardening, sewing, home repairs, cleaning — do it yourself. Basic cleaners are bicarbonate of soda for general cleaning — wash-basin and toilet. White vinegar puts a shine on tiles, and used on dampened newspaper cleans mirrors and shower screen and can be left overnight to clean the toilet. Ammonia can be used for shower tiles and screen also. Washing soda, Lectic soda with boiling water, clears blocked sinks.

It is good to listen to the golden oldies who have lived through the wars and depressions and built on their experience. At home children can be taught their alphabet, times table and how to add, subtract and multiply. The nursery rhymes and fairy stories are popular once more.

The best things in life are free — visiting, entertaining, singing, reading, playing bridge and other card games; doing crosswords, bush-walking, bicycling, picnics, barbecues. Other sports include swimming, tennis, horse riding, camping, golf, football, soccer and cricket. Entertainments are freely available, such as dining out, theatre, art galleries, concerts, musical evenings; browsing in antique shops, poetry readings, garden clubs, fashion parades, business seminars, study courses, discussion groups; clubs for photography, stamp collecting, and all other interests; dog training, murder/mystery weekends, and Yulefest in winter the highlight.

The next advice from the Nazis in Rumania to the Jewish population "You be responsible for your own murder!" also applies to the Muslims, Catholics, Orthodox and Christians trying to escape from the war in the Balkans. The two million and more Muslims murdered so far were not allowed to arm themselves. No murder, no way! In future self-defence in every way. Keep everything from now on, even a bit of 4 × 2 (4" × 2" timber) could come in handy one day. Keep the standards up and defend the quality and the quantity. Use imagination! Put oneself in the enemy's shoes and anticipate their next move.

Australians are known for resourcefulness. In the last war, communications with Europe on ham radio were carried out by rigging up aerials in gumtrees. While the satellite beams information, all is well. If not, we may have to go back to the crystal set.

On the money scene, already the 1 cent and 2 cent coins have been withdrawn. The plastic $5 note with metallic strip for monitoring is based on the Deutschmark leading to the ultimate electronic human marking, monitoring, re-educating as a race of robots controlled by a super power. Nazi German technology is already being set up around Australia. It would be good if we could dismantle this and send the enemy back defeated. No way! Like the good Germans, *"Nie wieder!" "Das Lamm wird sie überwinden." "Lobe den Herrn!" "Schöner Herr und Sterner König."* Compassion and concern for one another is growing everywhere. Thank goodness!

In the days of the Premier of New South Wales, Nicholas Greiner, Australians right around the coastline burned candles.

Australians are not hothouse flowers. The hardy wattle blooms forever.

Waratah and Wattle
by Henry Lawson

Though poor and in trouble I wander alone
    With a rebel cockade in my hat;
Though friends may desert me, and kindred disown,
    My country will never do that!
You may sing of the Shamrock, the Thistle and Rose,
    Or the three in a bunch if you will;
But I know of a country that gathered all those,
And I love the great land where the Waratah grows,
    And the Wattle bough blooms on the hill.

Australia! Australia! so fair to behold —
    While the blue sky is arching above,
The stranger should never have need to be told
That the Wattle bloom means that her heart is of gold,
    And the Waratah red blood of love.

Australia! Australia! most beautiful name
    Most kindly and bountiful land.
I would die every death that I might save her from shame
    If a black cloud should rise on the strand.
But whatever the quarrel, whoever her foes
    Let them come! Let them come when they will.
Though the struggle be grim, 'tis Australia that knows
That her children shall fight while the Waratah grows
    And the Wattle blooms out on the hill.

Sir Winston Churchill wanted a United States of Europe with Germany, and sanctioned Germany into NATO. At his death on 24th January 1965, he requested "The Battle Hymn of the Republic". He also deplored anti-Semitism maintaining

Jerusalem must be the ultimate goal. (*WINSTON CHURCHILL, A Brief Life* by Piers Brendon — 1984 Great Britain).

While the European Community and United Nations are preaching peace, One Woman's War goes on. In the words of Napoleon, quoted by Sir Winston Churchill "If you want peace, prepare for War".

BLUE MOUNTAINS' ECSTASY

The sunset falls on craggy walls
And mountain peaks old in story.
Cliff faces glow, in an endless row
And rosellas fly past in a blaze of glory.
Laugh! Kookaburra, laugh!
Fill the valleys with echoes.
Au revoir, radiant sun, *au revoir*,
As romantic evening mist follows.

Morning breaks and the magpie wakes
Carolling sweetly over the plain.
Currawongs calling, water falling,
Gumleaves sparkling in fragrant rain.
Chant cicadas, chant!
As bush insects join the choir.
Pulsate, warm earth, pulsate!
And set my heart on fire!

Crystal creek turns by gentle ferns,
Bright wattles bloom, vibrant gold.
Time erases on stark cliff faces
Furrows that tell stories of old.
Thunder, waterfall, thunder!
Splash the scampering wallaby!
Is this your heart that is calling?
Coo-ee! Coo-ee! Coo-ee!

(Inspired by Alfred Lord Tennyson's
THE PRINCESS: A Medley IV.)